# Abandoned

## Patricia H. Rushford

# *Books by Patricia Rushford*

## *Young Adult Fiction*

### JENNIE McGRADY MYSTERIES
1. *Too Many Secrets*
2. *Silent Witness*
3. *Pursued*
4. *Deceived*
5. *Without a Trace*
6. *Dying to Win*
7. *Betrayed*
8. *In Too Deep*
9. *Over the Edge*
10. *From the Ashes*
11. *Desperate Measures*
12. *Abandoned*
13. *Forgotten*

## *Adult Fiction*

*Morningsong*

### HELEN BRADLEY MYSTERIES
1. *Now I Lay Me Down to Sleep*
2. *Red Sky in Mourning*
3. *A Haunting Refrain*

# Abandoned

## Patricia H. Rushford

## BETHANY HOUSE PUBLISHERS
MINNEAPOLIS, MINNESOTA 55438

*Abandoned*
Copyright © 1999
Patricia Rushford

Cover illustration by Sergio Giovine
Cover design by the Lookout Design Group

Published by Bethany House Publishers
A Ministry of Bethany Fellowship International
11400 Hampshire Avenue South
Minneapolis, Minnesota 55438
www.bethanyhouse.com

Printed in the United States of America by
Bethany Press International, Minneapolis, Minnesota 55438

ISBN 0–7642–2120–5

Dedicated to
Kathryn and Noah

PATRICIA RUSHFORD is an award-winning writer, speaker, and teacher who has published numerous articles and more than thirty books, including *What Kids Need Most in a Mom*, *The Jack and Jill Syndrome: Healing for Broken Children*, and *Have You Hugged Your Teenager Today?* She is a registered nurse and has a master's degree in counseling from Western Evangelical Seminary. She and her husband, Ron, live in Washington State and have two grown children, eight grandchildren, and lots of nephews and nieces.

Pat has been reading mysteries for as long as she can remember and is delighted to be writing a series of her own. She is a member of Mystery Writers of America, Sisters in Crime, Romance Writers of America, and several other writing organizations. She is also the co-director of Writer's Weekend at the Beach.

# 1

"He's going to kill me." Jennie McGrady hurried down the hall to Mr. Baker's office. She was ten minutes late for her appointment to discuss her upcoming science project and to get next week's assignment.

"Jennie, wait up."

Jennie stopped at the door and turned toward the familiar voice. "Hi, Annie. What's up?"

Annie Phillips gave her a half smile and hurried toward her. Her shiny ink black hair bounced on her shoulders as she ran. "I need to talk to you."

Her blue gaze darted around the near empty hallway as though she was afraid of being overheard. Most of the kids were in classes, and Annie was obviously late for hers. She looked up at Jennie, who was about a head taller. "Do you have a minute?"

Jennie glanced inside the office, where Mr. Baker sat at his desk, waiting for her. "Not right now. I'm late. How about after school?" Jennie had planned on going home after her appointment, but Annie seemed eager to talk. "I could hang around for a while—I need to use the library anyway. I could give you a ride home."

"I was going to meet Shawn, but I guess I can see him later."

"We could get together tomorrow—"

"No! That may be too late. This is important. Allison said I should talk to you. She said if anyone could help, it would be you. Lisa told me the same thing."

"I thought I heard someone." Mr. Baker stepped out of his office and turned to Annie. "Did you need something? I have an appointment with Jennie right now, but I'll be glad to—"

"No. Um . . ." She flashed a hall pass. "I was just on my way to the office to pick up some papers for Mrs. Adams. I saw Jennie and stopped to say hello. I . . . I'd better go." Annie backed away. "I'll meet you out front after school, Jennie." She turned and hurried back in the direction she'd come.

Jennie stared after the petite figure. "She seems upset about something."

"I noticed that in class today. Probably nervous about whether she'll be elected Fall Festival Queen."

"Hmm." Jennie doubted that but didn't say so. What she'd seen in Annie's eyes was not anxiety about the possibility of her reigning over the fall festivities, but something far more serious. A lump settled in the pit of her stomach as her intuition started sending out warning signals. Jennie had no idea what Annie wanted to talk about. She did know one thing, though—Annie was afraid of something . . . or someone.

# 2

"Jennie?"

"Um . . . oh, right." Jennie reluctantly shifted her attention to the teacher. "Mr. Baker, I'm sorry I'm late. Nick is home sick today, and I had to stay with him until Mom came home. She was late coming back, and to top it off, there was a huge backup on the freeway by the Oregon City exit."

He laughed. "It's all right, Jennie. Your mother called and said you were running late. It's not a problem. I was just grading papers. Speaking of which . . ." He smiled, and his warm brown gaze twinkled from deep-set eyes on a narrow face. Mr. Baker had the lean look of a vegetarian—tall, with a lot of brain and not much muscle. "The one you did on acid rain was excellent."

"Thanks." Jennie ducked her head and smiled.

"I especially liked the interview with the head of the environmental agency. Nice touch. A lot of kids forget that they can use real people in their research."

"That was the fun part. I actually interviewed him on the Internet." Jennie's parents had finally given in to her request and set her up with a modem and an online service. She loved it, especially email.

"You really ought to think about going into the sciences, Jennie." He led her into his cramped office and sat in a cushioned executive chair with wheels, then motioned Jennie to sit in the worn but serviceable straight-backed wooden chair in front of the desk. A makeshift bookcase overflowed with reference books. Boxes of files sat on the floor waiting to be tucked into the three-drawer metal file cabinet. "You have a passion for this sort of thing."

Jennie shrugged and gave her usual answer. "I'll think about it." Though she enjoyed all of her subjects, her real passion was for law enforcement. She planned to become a lawyer and maybe someday a real detective. She loved the idea of following in her grandparents' and father's footsteps. They'd all worked in various law enforcement agencies. Her father had recently left the Drug Enforcement Agency and taken a job as a homicide detective with the Portland police.

"So, Jennie." Mr. Baker handed her the paper she'd aced and leaned forward, resting his thin arms on his desk. "What are your plans for the science project?"

"I'm doing it on fetal development. My mom is pregnant, so I thought I'd monitor her progress."

"Yes, I heard about that. How is she doing?"

"She had a few rough weeks with morning sickness and everything, but she's a lot better."

"Good. How are you feeling about the homeschool situation this year? Are you keeping up?"

"Sure."

"There was some talk about your coming to Trinity full time this year."

Jennie nodded. "It didn't work out. With Mom sick so much, she hasn't been able to work, so we just have Dad's income. Besides, Mom still needs my help with the house and Nick." Because Jennie's mother needed her at home, they had worked out a flexible program with the private school where Jennie would be partially homeschooled and would attend Trinity when she needed to be there for tests, lectures, special assignments, or meetings with various teachers.

"Are you happy with that?"

Jennie shrugged. "Yeah. Sometimes I miss out on things at school, but Lisa fills me in."

"Good. Now tell me about your science project. How are you planning to do your presentation?"

"Besides the fold-out display you suggested, I'll have actual models of a fetus in different stages of development. I've already talked to a friend of Mom's from a crisis pregnancy center. She said she would loan me a set of models. I'm planning to access a lot of the materials on the Internet and thought I'd interview Dr. Phillips too—if he has time."

"I'm sure he will. Paul Phillips is an excellent source for you. I hear he's one of the best pediatricians around. Your project sounds like it will be a good one. I trust you'll enter it in the City-Wide Science Fair." He opened a folder and pulled out a flyer. Handing it to her, he added, "It's not mandatory that you do, but I think with you and Gavin in the fair, Trinity High stands a good chance at taking home top honors."

"I don't know, Mr. Baker. I don't mind presenting it for the class, but doing it in front of judges—um . . . I'm not much of a speaker."

Disappointment flitted across his eyes. "Nonsense. You'll do a great job. Just pretend the judges are all students. And think of what winning will do for our school. We need to generate some excitement and build up morale. Losing the school and so many students has dampened spirits a bit."

The school and church had been destroyed in an arson fire, and Trinity High was now housed in a remodeled warehouse while their school was being rebuilt. The warehouse was adequate but not nearly as nice as their other facility had been. At any rate, Jennie kept reminding herself, at least they *had* a school. "Um . . . Mr. Baker, isn't it against the law to get your students to comply by making them feel guilty?" Jennie tossed him a teasing grin.

Her science teacher raised his eyebrows. "Not to my knowledge." A smile pulled at the corners of his mouth. "As they say, all's fair in love and science projects."

"I think that's 'love and war.' " She shook her head. "All right, I'll think about it. If it turns out really well, I might."

Jennie loved being an honor student, but she didn't especially like the extra pressure the teachers put on her. It didn't seem fair that they'd push you to greater heights when you were already on top. Fortunately, in this case she could say no without it affecting her grade. *Why fight it, McGrady?* she said to herself. *You know you're going to do it. Since when have you been able to walk away from a challenge?*

"I guess that'll have to do." Mr. Baker leaned back and tapped his pen on his knee. "I'll be glad to help in any way I can. I'd like to see your rough draft by next Friday. If you have any questions, give me a call."

"I will. Thanks." Jennie did a quick calculation. Today was Thursday. She had seven days. She also had a history test Friday, which meant she'd be working on the project most of the week-end.

"In case you do enter your project, you'll want the guide-lines." He handed Jennie another paper, which she briefly scanned and tucked into her backpack with her report and the first flyer.

Jennie made her way to the school office to pick up her mail. The wall of mailboxes was new to the students this fall. Rather than get handouts and miscellaneous notes and graded papers in class, the teachers and secretary would usually place them in the individual boxes. Jennie used the small key on her key chain and opened the metal door. Inside was a copy of their school paper, *The Trinity Tidings*, and a note from DeeDee, her coach, reminding her about the swim meet that afternoon at four-thirty. Jennie winced. She'd forgotten all about it. Not that it mattered much. She would have shown up for practice anyway.

"Hi, Jennie," Mrs. Talbot greeted as she eased her ample frame around her desk.

"Hey, Mrs. Talbot. How's the hip?" The secretary had been seriously injured in the fire and had spent nearly a month in ther-apy.

She offered Jennie a wide, dimpled smile. "Good as new. Got rid of my crutches a couple days ago. Doc says he's never seen anyone my age heal so fast. Told him it was the Lord's doing. Can I help you with something?"

"No. Just picking up my mail." She stuffed it away without looking at the rest.

"In that case, I may as well just give you this." She pulled a pink flyer from the stack in her hands. "It's for parents—a re-

minder about the work party for our rebuilding project Saturday."

Jennie deposited it in her backpack, thanked Mrs. Talbot,
and left. She got as far as her car before she remembered her
meeting with Annie. Ordinarily she would have gone straight to
the pool to swim laps. She glanced at her watch. School wouldn't
be out for another hour and a half. She sighed, unlocked the car,
pulled out her history text and a note pad, then tossed the bag
in the back.

"Might as well study," she mumbled. Taking her book back
into the school, she hurried down the long corridor to the library. Several students meandered about the small room or sat
in cubicles at computers. The shelves, what few of them they
had, were filled with books—all of them donated. Their beautiful library and several thousand books had been destroyed in
the fire. People had been generous, and in time many of the
books would be replaced. Even so, an ache returned to Jennie's
heart whenever she thought of the fire. Michael, the youth di-
rector and a good friend, had died from the severe burns he'd
received when he'd gone back into the burning building to res-
cue Mrs. Talbot and some of the others.

Jennie swallowed the lump in her throat and concentrated on
her notes for Friday's test.

When the bell rang, Jennie snapped her book shut and
headed for the door. By the time she'd made it through the
crowd, talked to several friends, told her cousin and best friend,
Lisa Calhoun, she'd see her at the swim meet, and paused for a
drink of water, Annie was already waiting.

"We'll have to hurry," Jennie said. "I forgot about the swim
meet this afternoon. I can take you home, or you can come to
the meet if you want."

"I'm not sure. I probably should just go home."

Shawn Conners, Annie's boyfriend, drove past them as they
approached Jennie's car. "Hey, Jen." He braked, then leaned out
the window of his black BMW and waved. "You're not forgetting
about the meet, are you?"

"Not a chance. You going?"

"Wouldn't miss it." He gave her a thumbs-up, then turned

to Annie. "I'll call you later, okay?"

Annie nodded. "Actually, I'll see you at the pool. Maybe you could take me home after?"

"Sure, no problem."

A couple toots on his horn and he drove out of the parking lot. Jennie unlocked the door, set her history book on the floor in the back, and climbed in. Though the temperature was in the midsixties, the intermittent sun had turned the car into an oven. Jennie opened her window and suggested Annie do the same.

Annie set her book bag on the floor between her feet and snapped her seat belt in place. She seemed angry about something.

"Want to talk about it?" Jennie asked.

"What. . . ?" Annie whipped back around to face Jennie. "I . . . that van over there. I think it's the one that's been following me. That's why I changed my mind about going home."

"Over where?" Jennie looked in the direction Annie pointed. There were a ton of vehicles coming and going. Parents picking kids up. Kids with their own cars driving out.

"That turquoise minivan across the street."

Jennie spotted it right away. "Any idea who it is?"

"No."

"Let's see if we can find out." Jennie eased into the line of traffic leaving the school, but instead of making her usual left, she went right so she could drive past the van in question. "Shoot, I can't see. The windows are tinted. Write down the license number and we'll check it out later."

Jennie checked the rearview mirror. The van had gone the opposite direction. "They're definitely not following us."

Annie released a long breath. "Maybe they didn't notice I was with you."

"Is that what you wanted to talk to me about? You think someone's been following you?"

Annie bit her lower lip. "Yes. It started after *The Oregonian* announced our Fall Festival celebration and ran the pictures of us. I got to thinking about the case you solved for Allison when she was on the Rose Festival Court. She said you might be able to find out who's been following me. I catch sight of the van every once in a while. Maybe the person isn't even driving that van. Maybe it's just that I notice it because it's such a bright color."

When Jennie made a left at the light, Annie put the sun visor down and fished in her bag for her sunglasses.

"Are you sure you're being followed?"

"Yes. You know the feeling you get when someone is watching you? I get chills up and down my spine. My hair feels like it's standing on end, and my stomach gets all tied up in knots."

Jennie took her own sunglasses from the holder on her visor and slipped them on. "Have you gotten any notes or strange phone calls?"

"No." She sighed. "Maybe I'm being paranoid. Shawn seems to think so. I don't have any proof or anything. It's just that I have this feeling. I was hoping maybe you would—you know, watch me leave school sometime to see if anyone is following me. I don't know." Annie turned in her seat. "Do you think you could help? I don't know what else to do."

"Have you talked to your parents or the police?" Jennie turned right again, setting them on a course that would take them to Lake Oswego, where their meet was being held and where their school had been. The only part of the school remaining, if fact, was the gymnasium and pool complex, which had been a separate building connected to the school by a long breezeway.

"What would I tell them? I have no proof. No one has tried to contact me."

Jennie pursed her lips. "There really isn't much I can do except check the license plate. In the meantime, it might help for you to keep a diary. Write down the times you feel like you're being watched. Maybe we can establish a pattern and do some watching ourselves."

"Thanks, Jennie. Somehow I knew you'd help."

"Do you mind if I ask Lisa to help too?"

"Not at all." She folded her arms. "I wouldn't be surprised if it was Charity. She hates me. I'm not sure why."

Jennie glanced over at Annie. "Charity? I'll admit she can be a pain, but I really doubt she'd go that far." Charity Brooks was nearly as tall as Jennie, but more filled out. Basically, she was gorgeous and knew it. Her golden hair had a spiral perm, and her skin glowed from a summer in the sun. "Does she have a teal minivan?"

"No—at least not that I know of. But she could be renting one."

"Not likely. She's too young."

"Well, maybe she borrowed it from someone." She sighed. "You're probably right. It's just that she seems so vindictive."

"You're not the only one running against her for Fall Festival Queen. What about Allison and Lisa?"

Annie tapped her long pink nails on the dash. "You have a point. If it was Charity, she'd probably be doing something to them too. I'm not sure if that makes me feel better. If it isn't Charity, then who?"

They drove in silence for a few minutes while they turned into the drive to Trinity's sports center. Jennie maneuvered down the narrow road, past the construction site of where the church and school used to be, and into the parking lot near the gym.

Annie turned to look at the new foundation. "I can't believe how far along they are. They've already poured the concrete."

"It's going a lot faster than I thought." Jennie glanced into her rearview mirror and whistled. "Don't look now, but that van you were so worried about is right behind us."

# 3

Annie closed her eyes tight and gripped the door handle. "I knew it. We're both going to die. I'm sorry I dragged you into this, Jennie."

"Get a grip, Annie. This is a public place with all kinds of people roaming around. Which makes it easier for me." Jennie pulled into a parking space and turned off the engine. "Where's that license plate number I asked you to write down?"

Annie handed her a neon pink Post-it Note. The van in question pulled into a spot several spaces down. "Stay here," Jennie cautioned. "It may not even be the same van. I'll check it out."

Jennie climbed out of the car and approached the teal blue van. It was the same license plate, all right. Jennie walked past the van, then stopped a short distance away, where she could get a view of the driver.

An attractive, dark-haired woman wearing sunglasses, a pin-striped suit, and high heels scooted out, then leaned back in to get something from the front passenger seat. She pulled out a black briefcase, secured the strap over her shoulder, pocketed her keys, and closed the door.

Instead of going inside, she walked over to another vehicle—a brown station wagon—then waited for a man with a video camera. Jennie smiled. Annie was definitely imagining things. She hurried back to her own car to give Annie the good news.

"It's okay. I don't think you're in any danger from the driver of *that* van. It's Debra Noble from Channel 22 News. She's probably here to cover the meet."

"Really? Debra Noble?" Annie's face lit up. "She's so cool."

"You've met her?"

"Uh-huh. She interviewed Lisa, Allison, Charity, and me when we were chosen to run for Fall Festival Queen."

"Right. Lisa mentioned that. I wondered at the time why they'd bother with Trinity—we're not that big a school."

"She tied it in to our school spirit and how we're coming back so strong after the fire. People are interested in that sort of thing. I'll bet that's why she's here. Maybe to let everyone know how we're doing and that we're not giving up. We still have a long way to go, of course, but the community and the church have worked really hard. Whenever she talks about us, she tells people they can send donations to the trust fund. Dad says it's good to keep the story in the news. That way we not only keep getting donations, but we also get volunteers to work on the rebuilding."

Jennie nodded. "Well, I guess that part of your mystery is solved. If she's keeping track of what's going on at Trinity, it's no wonder you see her van a lot."

*Of course, there are others like it,* Jennie reminded herself. *Teal is a popular color.* While she wanted to ease Annie's mind, Jennie still had not dismissed the possibility that someone other than Debra could be driving a similar van, and that person could be following, or stalking, Annie Phillips. Or Annie could be making the whole thing up to bring attention to herself. Jennie canceled the thought. Annie's eyes held a genuine look of fear.

"So, Annie," Jennie said, "do you feel like someone's watching you now, or can you relax for a while and enjoy the meet?"

Her cheeks dimpled in a deep smile. "I'm feeling much better now that I know you're on the case."

Jennie let the comment slide. She didn't consider this a *case* by any stretch of the imagination—at least not yet. She did, however, want to pursue the matter. "Good. Listen, I've got to go, but I have a plan for tomorrow after school. I'll talk to you later."

"Great. Thanks, Jennie."

They entered the building with Annie making a beeline for the bleachers, where Shawn and several of his friends were sitting. Jennie squeezed through the crowd, surprised at the number of students and parents there. The meet was the first of the season.

18

They were facing their biggest rival, Riverside Heights, the largest private school in the area. Trinity had been the largest until the fire. Not wanting to go to school in a remodeled warehouse and being afraid that Trinity had been targeted by extremist groups, a lot of kids had transferred. Trinity may have lost a few students, but they were determined to come back stronger than ever. Jennie felt a fierce sense of pride. If they could win against Riverside, maybe they could make it to the state championships.

Butterflies fluttered in Jennie's stomach. She hauled in a deep breath and blew it out through her mouth. Competition like this was new to her. She'd often raced against friends, but only for fun. *This will be fun too*, she told herself. *You just have to concentrate on swimming and forget about the crowds and the cameras.*

"Nervous?"

Jennie's thoughts and feet came to an abrupt halt. Gavin nearly ran into her. Gavin Winslow was a good friend and the editor of the school paper. He was about her height—five eight, gangly, and cute in a Clark Kent sort of way.

"No." She eyed his poised camera with disdain. "You're not going to take pictures of me again, are you?"

"Photos, Jennie. How many times do I have to tell you? They're photos." He grinned and pushed his glasses back to the bridge of his nose. "I might take some later. Did you know you are favored to win the 500? Coach Dayton says if you swim at the meets like you do in practice—"

"Did you need something?" she interrupted. She did know about the stats. DeeDee was expecting a lot from her, which did nothing to calm her butterflies. She didn't want to hear about her potential again. It just added more pressure. Jennie didn't know if she could swim under pressure. "I have to change."

"I just wanted to wish you luck." His eyes held a slightly injured look.

"Thanks. Look, I'm sorry I snapped at you."

"No problem. You got first-meet jitters like everyone else."

"Yeah . . . I guess."

"Well, you've got nothing to worry about."

"Except for the fact that I might blow it. What if I freeze up?"

"You won't." He squeezed her shoulder. "I have faith in you."

"That's good, because I don't have much in myself at the moment."

"Jennie—I . . ." Gavin's gaze met hers. "There's something . . ." He looked away. "Never mind. We can talk about it later. You'd better get ready." He turned and walked away.

*Grrr.* She hated it when people didn't finish telling you what they started. *This is not the time to dwell on it, McGrady. You've got a swim meet to think about. Besides, it probably isn't that important.* Somehow Jennie couldn't quite convince herself of that. *Later. You can deal with Gavin and Annie's problems later.* Right now she had to concentrate on getting into her swimsuit and at least making an appearance. As weak as her knees were getting, Jennie wasn't sure she'd have the strength to do even that.

---

An hour later, Jennie stood on the block, preparing herself for the 500 meter. She shook her hands and arms, then adjusted her goggles. The silence just before a heat was nearly as deafening as the cheers that had gone up for the last winner. She reached up and adjusted her swim cap, tucking in a strand of hair she'd missed. *I'm going to be sick.*

*No, you're not!* Jennie pursed her lips and sucked in a deep breath. *Ready.* She poised herself.

A gunshot exploded through the stillness, scattering her butterflies and sending her adrenaline into another time zone. Jennie's slim form sliced into the water without a splash. So far so good.

Before the meet had officially started, Coach Dayton told them they shouldn't focus so much on winning as on technique and endurance. "Get the job done. I'm not looking for big-time heroes. I'm looking for a strong team."

Jennie was a strong swimmer, and she knew it. At her first turn, she was out in front by several seconds. The 500 meter was Jennie's best event. She'd already raced in the relay. Trinity had lost, but by only half a second. She'd watched the men's relay and the first segment of diving. So far they were ahead in total points. By the second turn the butterflies and anxiety were gone. Could she push them even farther into the lead?

*Don't think about that,* Jennie reminded herself. *Not yet. Dolphins. Think dolphins.* Jennie closed her mind to the shouts and whistles coming from the stands and to the swimmers on either side of her. She recalled her glorious weeks in Florida swimming with the sleek and beautiful creatures, racing to keep up with them. Cutting through the water effortlessly, she pursued the dolphins in her mind.

She would go at the pace she'd set until the last turn, then push harder. Though she tried not to think that much about winning, she couldn't stop the desire rising within her. She had always been a fierce competitor. Now was no different.

When she hit the wall for the last time, she knew she'd won by over half a lap. The only real competitor was her own teammate Kelly Mason, a junior. They gave each other a high five.

Jennie took her time getting out of the pool. Knowing Gavin, he'd be taking "photos." As much as Jennie loved winning, she didn't much like the attention. She pulled off her goggles and swim cap and glanced toward the stands. Sure enough, Gavin had his camera focused on her and Kelly. Kelly hung an arm around Jennie's shoulder. "Nice job, Jen."

"Thanks. You too."

With her part finished, Jennie relaxed, and after drying off and slipping on her sweats, she sat with her teammates, watching the diving competition and occasionally stealing glances at the crowd and at Annie.

Annie and Shawn sat together looking as normal as ever. The TV reporter was squatting down on the floor talking to a man in the front row. Jennie did a double take. *Dad?* She hadn't expected either of her parents to show up for the meet. But there they were in the front row. Her mom, Susan, her brother, Nick, and her dad, Jason. Right behind them sat Lisa and her family. Jennie's aunt Kate and uncle Kevin, Lisa and her little brother, Kurt. Lisa, Nick, and Kurt waved at her, and Jennie waved back, pleased that they'd all come. But why shouldn't they? They were a close family, with Lisa more like a sister than a cousin. Aunt Kate was Jennie's dad's twin sister. Kate's husband, Kevin, was

Jennie's mom's brother. Which explained why Jennie looked so much like Kate, and Lisa resembled Jennie's mom.

How like them to surprise her like that. She wondered why she hadn't seen them earlier. Jennie blamed it on nerves.

Mom, Aunt Kate, and Uncle Kevin were looking at Debra Noble. Dad didn't seem very happy with the reporter, but he kept talking to her. At that moment, Jennie would have given anything to have bionic ears so she could eavesdrop. Were they talking about the meet or one of Dad's cases? He was a homicide detective for the Portland police.

Jason McGrady held up a hand and shook his head, motioning toward the diving platform. Debra pointed to Jennie and smiled. The cameraman swung away from Dad, panned the swim team, then rested on Jennie. She pretended not to notice, focusing instead on the student approaching the diving board.

When Jennie glanced back at her dad, the reporter had moved away. She, too, was looking at the senior Russ Cassidy, who was getting ready for his next dive.

Jennie watched as Russ adjusted his stance on the end of the board. He balanced there, his back to the water. After several seconds of heart-stopping silence, he shot high into the air, tucked, executed three turns, straightened, then knifed into the water. Perfect.

Jennie's voice joined those of the other Trinity students, and for the next half hour she cheered her teammates on to victory. After the meet, Jennie gladly listened to the accolades of her proud family; then she talked briefly with Debra Noble, but only after the woman stuck a microphone in her face.

"How does it feel to be a winner, Jennie?"

Jennie laughed. "Great. Trinity's the best! But you shouldn't be talking to me. Coach Dayton deserves the credit." Behind her the kids were waving and cheering.

"Between you and your father, McGrady is getting to be a household name in this town."

Jennie shrugged, wondering where Debra was going with the interview. Jennie had made the news several times lately in connection with some high-profile investigations.

"You helped the police track down the arsonist responsible

for burning down your church and school. A couple of months back you rescued your little brother from kidnappers. And that's only the beginning," Debra said. "I understand you're an honor student. Now you're breaking records for your swim team. Is there anything you *don't* do?"

"I don't answer stupid questions." Heat crept up Jennie's neck and into her face as she realized she'd made the comment aloud. She had no idea what had possessed her to be so rude. Reporters could be so annoying.

Debra laughed. "My, you *do* take after your father, don't you?"

Jennie didn't know how to answer that. Apparently Debra wasn't expecting her to, as she went on to congratulate Jennie. "You and your teammates did a terrific job out there today."

"Um . . . thanks."

Debra turned toward the camera. Jennie tuned her out, hoping she'd cut Jennie's sarcastic remark if any of the footage made it to the news broadcast.

"I'm proud of you, princess." Dad hooked an arm around her neck and hugged her to him. Jennie hugged him back.

"You did a great job." Mom hugged her as well.

"What do you say we all celebrate with pizza?"

"Are you sure you can take the time?" Uncle Kevin asked sarcastically, then snickered as if they were sharing some kind of inside joke.

"What was that all about?" Jennie asked.

Kate frowned at Debra and the cameraman, who were now focused on Russ Cassidy. "That woman had the nerve to ask your father why he was here watching a swim meet and not out trying to find that serial killer."

"You can't blame her, Kate," Dad said. "She wants an end to it. There was another murder last night."

Jennie looked at her dad. "Another pro-life victim?"

"I'm afraid so."

Jennie frowned. It was the third such killing in two weeks. The first had been a woman who had recently spearheaded an anti-abortion bill. The second was a man who routinely picketed abortion clinics in the area. Notes had been left on the bodies of both victims with a radical pro-choice group taking credit. The issue had created a political firestorm. Pro-choice advocates claimed to know nothing about it and blamed pro-lifers for killing their own so the pro-choice groups would look bad. The pro-life groups argued that the pro-choice people were showing their true colors. After all, if they sanctioned the murder of unborn babies, they were murderers.

"Let's not talk about that now," Jennie's mom insisted. "I think pizza is a great idea—especially now that I can eat it without throwing up."

Jennie picked up Nick, who'd been tugging at her towel. "I'm surprised to see you here. Thought you were sick."

"My tummy's all better. Mom said I could come and watch you swim."

"I'm glad you did."

That night Jennie had trouble sleeping. Questions about Annie and Gavin kept clogging her brain. Gavin had wanted to talk to her about something, but he hadn't called. Maybe it wasn't all that important. She punched her pillow and turned on the lamp, then picked up her newest mystery and settled down to read.

After school on Friday, Jennie hurried to her locker, picked up the books she'd need over the weekend, and went straight to her car. Lisa met her there.

"You ready for our stakeout?" Lisa asked.

"I guess." She glanced toward the entrance of the school, where Shawn and Annie waited in Shawn's BMW. "Let's go." Jennie slid into the driver's seat and leaned across the passenger seat to unlock the door. Once they'd both fastened their seat belts, Jennie started the car, released the emergency brake, and merged with the other cars. She took a right, went two blocks, then made a U-turn and came back. She parked in the shade of a large maple about half a block from the school, facing in the direction Annie and Shawn would eventually drive.

While Jennie drove, Lisa pulled two pairs of binoculars out from under the seat. When Jennie stopped, she handed her a pair.

They didn't have to wait long. Shawn pulled out of the parking lot, eased into the center lane, and made a left turn.

"No one seems to be following them." Lisa peered through the glasses.

"I think that's about to change." A beige sedan pulled out of a side street. The driver was a woman with a large mass of blond curls and wearing sunglasses. When Shawn turned at the next corner, the woman followed. Jennie's pulse accelerated. "Looks like Annie may have been right after all."

"You think that's our stalker?"

"Only one way to find out. Let's go." Jennie set the binoculars on the seat beside her. She had to let three cars pass before she could pull into the traffic lane. She wasn't worried, though. She and Shawn had worked out a route earlier. When Jennie got to Birch Street, she made a right. The other cars had gone straight. Shawn, having driven more slowly than usual, sat at a light ready to make a left turn onto Douglas Road. The woman was right behind him.

Jennie pulled up into the left-turn lane just as the green arrow showed. The woman glanced into the rearview mirror. Jennie tried to act nonchalant as she attempted to make out the woman's features.

"Did you get the license number?" she asked Lisa.

"Of course. And the make and model."

"Good." Being this close, Jennie could see that the car was an older Cadillac Seville.

The driver of the Caddy made her left turn, then suddenly moved into the right lane of traffic and made a quick right turn.

"Look." Lisa pointed. "She's going into the mall. I guess she wasn't following Annie after all."

Jennie chewed on the inside of her cheek. "Maybe. Or maybe we got too close and scared her off."

"Should we follow her?"

"No. We've got what we need. I'll ask Dad to have the DMV run a check on it. We should have a name by the end of the day."

# 4

"Oh," Jennie crooned, "Lisa, look. It's so-o-o cute." Jennie studied the photo of the developing fetus that was about the size of the tiny baby tucked safely away in her own mother's uterus. With Mom being pregnant and Jennie wanting to follow the baby's progress every step of the way, doing a science project on the subject seemed the most practical way to satisfy her curiosity and get credit at the same time. She thought again about Mr. Baker's suggestion that she enter it in the Science Fair. Maybe she would. She'd been on the Internet since eight A.M.—it was now ten-thirty—pulling in resources and gathering information. She'd had to wade through a lot of advertising and questionable resources, but she'd also found a lot of great material.

Lisa peered over Jennie's shoulder. Her wispy red curls tickled Jennie's face. "That is so cool. I wish I were doing my project on something like this instead of on tornadoes." Lisa had arrived only minutes before, wanting Jennie to go with her to the Clackamas Town Center Mall.

"Tornadoes are interesting." Jennie glanced at her cousin, then turned back to the computer screen.

"They're scary. I had no idea it would be so depressing. People die in those things." Lisa straightened and lifted a mass of coppery curls off her neck. "I guess I should get to work on it. Maybe after the meeting."

"What meeting?"

"Didn't I tell you?" Lisa wandered over to the dresser and lifted a plastic six-month fetus out of one of the models the woman at the nearby crisis pregnancy center had loaned Jennie. "B.J. said Gavin wants to meet us at the mall today. She said it was important and that Gavin especially wants you there."

"Why?"

"I think he needs your detective skills. Something strange has been going on in the journalism room at school. They've had stuff disappear. Thursday night someone broke into the main computer and totally messed up an article for the paper."

Jennie frowned. The school paper was Gavin's pride and joy. No wonder he was upset. "Maybe we can meet them tomorrow after church. I need to get a birthday card and present for Ryan."

"You're getting him a gift?"

Jennie cringed. So much for keeping her plans a secret. "Why not?"

"I can't believe you're still talking to him after he broke up with you like that."

"He's a friend, Lisa. He always will be."

"You still like him, don't you?" Lisa's smile lit her green eyes.

"Of course. I told you, he's a friend." Jennie didn't want to talk about Ryan. His decision to date another girl still hurt. She hadn't talked with him for nearly two weeks now. Their last conversation had been slightly less than friendly. Ryan had been as upset about her announcement to date Scott Chambers as she'd been about his going out with Camilla. Not that it mattered all that much. Jennie wasn't ready for a serious relationship with either guy. Or with anyone, for that matter. She had school and a career in law enforcement to think about.

Still, she didn't want to lose Ryan as a friend. Maybe sending him a birthday card would smooth things over. She hoped so.

"Are you going to take it to him personally?" Lisa asked in a teasing tone.

"Hey, that's not a bad idea. Maybe we could . . ." Jennie sighed. "But I can't. There's no way I can go this weekend, and his birthday is Wednesday." Ryan lived in Bay Village, on the Oregon Coast, next door to Jennie's grandmother. She didn't often have the opportunity to see him during the school year. She had to admit, though, that a visit to Gram and her new grandfather, J.B., was long overdue.

"So you could be a couple days late." Lisa ran a finger over the smooth finish of the pre-born figure in her hand. "We could all drive down to see Gram next weekend. Mom's been saying she needed to get down there."

"My folks have too. I really can't, though, Lisa." Jennie backed down. Sending the present and card would be best. It would be too awkward if he was still seeing Camilla.

"Whatever." Lisa gave her a knowing look and settled the model fetus back in its plastic womb.

"Good-bye," the computerized voice said as the program went offline.

Jennie waited for the sign-off to be completed, then clicked on the incoming mail and opened her latest email.

The message was from Gavin. He'd titled it "Urgent."

*Jennie, I'm in trouble. Get off the phone and call me!* was all it said.

"How rude." Lisa read the message over Jennie's shoulder. "What do you think he wants?"

Jennie shrugged. "He's probably going to issue me a personal invitation to his meeting."

Lisa made a face. "B.J. didn't say, but I'll bet it's the article he wrote about us."

"What article?" Jennie reached for the phone and dialed Gavin's number.

"Didn't I tell you? Oh, I was going to and we started talking about Ryan. I think that's what the meeting is all about. Don't tell me you didn't read it!" Lisa flopped on Jennie's bed and picked up a stuffed long-eared bunny out of Jennie's menagerie. "It was awful."

"Hello?" Gavin answered before Jennie could respond to Lisa's question. Jennie felt like a Ping-Pong ball being batted from one side of the net to the other.

"Hi," Jennie said. "What did you want?"

"It's about time," Gavin growled.

"Excuse me?" Jennie felt like slamming the phone in his ear. "What *is* your problem?"

"I'm sorry I yelled. I've been trying to call you all morning."

"I've been working on my science project." Jennie glanced at her cousin, who was sitting on her bed mouthing something Jennie couldn't understand. "What's wrong, Gavin?"

"Things are getting out of hand, and I need your help. Have you read the school paper?" Gavin sounded near panic.

"No. I had other things on my mind Friday and forgot to read my mail. Besides, I can't go anywhere right now." She had no idea what things Gavin was talking about and wasn't sure she wanted to know. "I have to work on my rough draft for science."

"What do you mean, you can't?" Gavin's voice broke as his volume increased. "Didn't you hear me? I need your help. It's a matter of life and death. You've got to help me find the person who wrote that article."

"So hire a detective." Jennie shifted the phone to her other ear and held it in place with her shoulder.

"Jennie, I'm dying here."

Jennie didn't need another complication in her life right now. She was already trying to track down Annie's stalker. Unfortunately, she'd had no luck yet with the license number. Her dad had taken it with him to work this morning but hadn't gotten back to her.

Even though she fought against it, she knew she'd end up helping Gavin. He was, after all, a friend. "Oh, come on, Gavin. It can't be that bad."

"It's bad. Everybody's mad at me. Mrs. Andrews is threatening to give me detention and give my job on the paper to someone else. But I didn't do it." He paused. "Hang on a sec—I got a call coming in on the other line."

"What did he say?" Lisa asked.

"Said he didn't do it. Whatever 'it' is. Do you have a copy of the school paper? I was so into finding Annie's stalker yesterday that I forgot to read it."

"Yeah, I do." Lisa rummaged through her bag and pulled it out. "It's the article about all the Fall Festival Queen contestants, isn't it? He had no right to go tabloid on us. Some of the stuff isn't even true. If he meant it as a joke, it isn't funny."

"Gavin says he's in big trouble."

"I can see why."

Jennie took the crumpled paper from Lisa and unfolded it.

The paper was a small one—two 11 × 17 pages folded in half.

"It's inside on page three," Lisa said.

On the inside right-hand page was an article entitled "Fall Festival Profiles." Each of the girls in the running for queen had been featured. The article gave some stats on them—GPA, hobbies, interests—and included a photo. That part was okay. It was the bold print under each segment that made Jennie cringe. Within each of the girls' frames was a caption labeled "Dirt." Under Lisa's it talked about her "problem with anorexia." Allison's mentioned how she'd "wet the bed until she was twelve." Charity Brooks "got a D in math last year and had to go to summer school." Annie's read, "Annie Phillips was a trash can baby."

"This is awful." Jennie sank onto her bed next to her cousin.

"It's worse than that," Lisa said. "Annie's especially. For the rest of us it's not so bad. Everybody knew about my problem. Allison confessed the bed-wetting thing at a slumber party last year. And it's no big secret about Charity's math grade either. But Annie's is really sick."

Scanning the rest of the article, Jennie read that Annie Phillips, one of Trinity High's most popular students, had been adopted as an infant by Dr. Paul Phillips and his wife, Jeanette. The writer of the article called Annie a piece of trash because Annie's real parents had thrown her away. "I didn't know Annie was adopted."

"She didn't either. She says it isn't true. She's threatening to sue Gavin for libel."

"I can see why Gavin is so upset." As the editor of the paper, he'd be credited with having written or okaying the article. He'd said he didn't do it, and Jennie believed him. Gavin was an honest person and a good reporter. He wouldn't print anything without the facts and research to back himself up. Even though the article brought up negative things about each of the girls, the piece on Annie was the worst. It looked as though someone was targeting her. Could it be the same person who'd been following her?

"Even if Gavin had known about Annie being adopted, he'd never have gone along with printing something that would be so hurtful to her," Jennie went on. "Who else has access to the journalism room besides Mrs. Andrews and Gavin?"

"B.J. You don't think B.J. might have done it?"

"Maybe a couple of months ago, when she first came to live with her dad, but not now."

Bethany Beaumont, who insisted on being called B.J., worked on the paper with Gavin. Her sister, Allison, was one of the girls running for Fall Festival Queen against Annie. B.J. definitely had an attitude problem at times, but who wouldn't with all she'd been through? She'd lost her mom and been thrown into a family she didn't even know existed until her mother's death.

"I know she can be a pain, but she wouldn't be this mean."

"I don't think so either." Jennie frowned. "Besides, I have a hunch this was written to hurt Annie more than any of the others. And as far as I know, B.J. likes Annie."

"Jennie?" Gavin came back on the line.

"Yeah—I'm still here. I just read the article. It's terrible. Who would have done something like this?"

"I don't know. I'm getting the blame. But never mind that. I just got a call from Mrs. Andrews. Annie is missing."

# 5

"Meet me at the mall in an hour," Gavin said. "I'll call B.J. and Allison again and tell them what time."

"You don't need me to pick you up?" Jennie asked. Gavin lived out in the country and didn't have a license or a car.

"No. I'll catch a ride with Mom. Might need you to take me home, though."

"No problem. Um . . . I might be a little late. I'd like to stop over at Annie's house. See if I can find out anything."

"Good idea. I'd go myself, but I don't think they'd welcome me right now. Can you let them know it wasn't me?"

"Sure." Jennie wrapped the phone cord around her finger. "We'd better go. . . ."

"We?"

"Lisa's here."

"Oh." Silence. "Tell her . . . tell her I didn't print that stuff about her, okay?"

"I will."

Jennie hung up, turned to her cousin, and repeated the conversation while they gathered their things and went downstairs.

Jennie leaped off the two bottom stairs, opened the front door, then closed it again. "Oops, my keys. And I'd better let Mom know where I'm going.

"Mom? Where are you?" Jennie yelled.

"In the kitchen."

Jennie and Lisa crossed the entry, then traipsed through the dining room and into the kitchen. Mom brushed her hand across her forehead, lifting her moist auburn bangs.

Mom looked especially pretty. Her cheeks were pink—a good sign. She'd also gained weight. Her pregnancy was barely visible under the loose cotton dress she wore.

"You look warm," Jennie said. "Are you feeling okay?"

"I am warm, but otherwise I feel great. Managed to keep my breakfast down this morning. I think I'll live through this."

"Good. Lisa and I are going out for a while."

"I thought you were going to get your rough draft done today." Susan McGrady took the spoon out of the blue Jell-O and tossed it in the sink.

"I was." Jennie explained the incident about the article that had mysteriously appeared in the school paper. "I don't know if I can do anything about it, but I really need to try."

"May I see the article?"

Jennie handed her the paper. "Annie is really upset. Gavin says she's missing. What makes matters even worse is that she's sure someone has been following her. I just hope whoever it was hasn't abducted her or something."

"Does your father know?

"I tried to call him, but he's out on a case. If he calls back, maybe you can tell him. And ask him about the license number I gave him last night. There may be a connection between that number and Annie's disappearance. In the meantime, Lisa and I are going to stop by Annie's house, then meet Gavin and B.J. at the mall. We have to try to find her and figure out what's going on."

Jennie's mom frowned as she read the article. "This is unthinkable. I can't believe the Phillipses never told her."

"You mean it's true?" Lisa asked. "She really was found in the trash?"

"I'm afraid so. I don't remember all the details, but I do remember the case. Kate and I talked about it at length. Being brand-new moms, we were horrified that anyone could throw away a precious baby. You two were only a few weeks old when it happened. Dr. Phillips was on duty at the hospital when the ambulance brought Annie in. She'd been born prematurely and nearly died. As far as I know, the police were never able to find the birth mother."

"How did they find Annie?"

"The police received an anonymous tip from a woman who said she heard a baby crying near the store where the trash bin was sitting."

"You mean she actually heard the baby and didn't stop? I can't believe anyone could be that cruel." Jennie frowned. "Unless she's the one who put her there."

"That's what the police thought. They figured the woman who called was the baby's mother."

"I'm glad someone got to Annie in time," Lisa said.

"Yes." Mom handed the paper back to Jennie. "I should call Jeanette and Paul. I'll put the family on the prayer chain."

"Good idea." Jennie grabbed the keys from the peg by the back door.

"Call me if you hear anything," Mom said.

"I will."

Jennie opened the door and glanced around. "Where are Nick and Bernie? Seems awfully quiet around here this morning." Bernie was Nick's oversized St. Bernard pup. They could both be a nuisance, but she loved them.

"I figured since you were going to be doing homework today, you might want it quiet. I had your dad drop Nick off at Kate's to play with Kurt, who insisted they bring Bernie. Honestly, sometimes I think he's better suited to Bernie than Nick. Nick rarely plays with him anymore."

"Bernie does play kind of rough. He practically knocks me over. Poor Nick ends up on his rear every time Bernie jumps up on him. Maybe you should give Bernie to Kurt. Nick doesn't take care of him like he should, and if he's afraid of him . . ."

"That's exactly what your father said this morning. I think it's a good idea—if Kate will go along with it."

"Mom would love it, and Kurt would be thrilled," Lisa said. "The hardest part would be convincing Nick."

"I think Jason was going to talk to him about the possibility this morning. We'll see how it goes. Bernie's just gotten too big for Nick to handle. I was thinking we might do better with a smaller pet that's easier to care for. A cat, maybe."

"Sounds good, Mom. We'd better go." Jennie pushed Lisa out the door. "Gavin will be waiting."

"You'll be back for dinner, won't you?" Mom called after her.

"Should be." Jennie turned around at the door. "I'll call you if I'm held up." Jennie and Lisa hurried to the car.

"Do you believe Gavin, Jennie?" Lisa asked. "I mean, who else could have done it? He's usually the first one in the journalism room in the morning and the last one to leave in the afternoon. Mrs. Andrews keeps it locked. He's the only student with a key."

"Yes, but he's in and out." Jennie tossed her bag into the backseat and eased her long, slender frame behind the wheel. "Mr. Schultz has a key."

Lisa gave her an odd look. "You suspect the janitor?"

"No, of course not. I'm just thinking about possibilities. But he might have let someone in." She pursed her lips. "If I wanted to get into the journalism room, how would I do it? I could get hold of one of the keys and have a duplicate made. Or I could hide in the journalism room before Mrs. Andrews locked up for the night. It would be easy enough to do."

"There are also heating vents. Whoever did it could have gotten into the ducts in another room and crawled over, then dropped down out of the vent."

"Hmm. Not my choice, but it is possible. Maybe Gavin can shed some light on it. We know he was at the swim meet Thursday after school. Did he run the results of the meet?"

Lisa flipped to the back of the paper. "Yep. Here's your picture and Russ's."

Jennie wrinkled her nose. "It's a 'photo.' I wish he wouldn't do that."

"Why not?" Lisa giggled. "You look cute with goggles on."

Jennie glanced at Lisa. "Don't tell me—not the goggles."

Lisa held the paper up so Jennie could see it.

Jennie groaned. "I'm going to kill him." Jennie's anger abated. *It's just the sports page,* she told herself. And appearing in the paper looking like an alien was not nearly as bad as what happened to Annie and the others.

They pulled into Annie's driveway fifteen minutes later. A

police car sat at the curb. The front door of the house was open, and a police officer stood just inside. "I'm sorry, ma'am. Doesn't look like she's in the neighborhood. Do you have a list of her friends? People she might have called or gone to visit?"

"Yes" came a tearful response.

The police officer apparently heard Jennie and Lisa approach and turned around to face them. A look of recognition, then surprise lit his blue eyes.

Jennie's stomach tightened. Her heart skipped. "Rocky! Um . . . hi." Her first impulse had been to hug him, but she didn't. He didn't look at all like he'd welcome that kind of familiarity.

He nodded. "Why am I not surprised to see you two here? I take it you're friends of Annie's?" Rocky, aka Dean Rockwell, had been involved in several investigations in which Jennie had played a part. He didn't welcome her help, and she didn't appreciate his macho attitude, but they'd developed a friendship of sorts over the course of the summer.

"We go to the same school."

He looked at her a moment, then said, "What do you know about this?"

Jennie shrugged. "Not much."

Mrs. Phillips opened the door wider. "Oh, Jennie. I just spoke to your mother on the phone. Thanks for coming. I'm trying to make a list of Annie's friends—maybe you and Lisa can help."

Rocky stepped aside and let them in.

The house was elegant—like the kind you'd find on the Street of Dreams. It had vaulted ceilings and a large flagstone entry. A rock planter and waterfall graced one side, and a wide, curved stairway led to the second floor. Jeanette Phillips led them to the dining room table, where she sat down in front of a yellow legal pad on which she'd written some names.

"We're so sorry, Mrs. Phillips," Lisa said.

"I'm sorry too. I can't believe Annie would run away like that."

"She ran away?" Jennie asked.

"She must have. I've never seen her so upset. We tried to reason with her, but she was terribly angry."

"Gavin says he's sorry the story about Annie's adoption got

into the paper. He wanted you to know that he didn't write it and is trying to find out who did."

"I'd like to know who's responsible and why they would dig up this information after all these years. I don't blame Gavin, though. It's my fault for keeping it a secret. Paul wanted to tell her she was adopted, but the time was never right." She rubbed at the goose bumps on her arms. "Now it may be too late."

"When did she leave?" Jennie asked.

"Last night. She was with Shawn and . . . I thought she'd cool off and come back, but she was gone all night."

Jennie sat in the chair next to Lisa and across from Mrs. Phillips. "Have you called Shawn?"

"Yes—this morning. I didn't talk to him directly. His mother told me that he'd gotten home a few minutes after eleven. He told them how upset Annie had been. I guess he talked to her for quite some time. She seemed to have things pretty well together when he dropped her off."

"So she came back here, then left again?" Jennie tossed Lisa a worried look.

"I guess so. According to Emily—Mrs. Conners, Shawn dropped Annie off here at eleven. But she never came inside. I never saw her."

"Where is Shawn now?" Jennie wondered why Rocky hadn't stopped her from asking all those questions. He'd undoubtedly heard the story before. Maybe he thought Mrs. Phillips would remember something else if she went over it again.

"He and his father have gone fishing up near Mount St. Helens. Emily says there's no way to contact them—unless they call her from a pay phone."

Lisa grabbed Jennie's arm. "Maybe Annie didn't run away after all. Maybe someone was watching and took her after Shawn dropped her off."

"I was thinking the same thing." Jennie blew out a long breath and glanced at Rocky, who was still standing by the table. "You might want to sit down," she said. "There's something you should know."

# 6

Rocky pulled a small notebook out of his pocket and sat down next to Jennie. "Okay, what have you got?"

"Mrs. Phillips," Jennie began, "did Annie say anything to you about someone following her?"

She shook her head and rubbed her forehead. "No. Are you saying. . . ?" Her panicky gaze swung from Jennie to Rocky, then back again. "If you don't think she ran away, then . . . what? You think she was taken—kidnapped?"

"I don't know. It's a possibility. Thursday afternoon she stopped me in the hall at school and told me she needed to talk. She was afraid someone was stalking her."

Jennie glanced at Rocky. "I asked her if she'd talked to the police or her parents, and she said she hadn't because she didn't have any proof. She said she'd feel stupid saying something, then being wrong. So after school yesterday, Lisa and I watched her and Shawn leave the school. A beige-colored Caddy came off a side street and followed them for a few blocks, then turned off. I'm thinking maybe she noticed that Lisa and I were behind her. We got the license plate number."

"I'd like to see it." Rocky held out his hand.

"Um . . ." Jennie stared at his open palm, then shifted her gaze to his sky-blue eyes. "I don't have it, and I can't remember what it is. I gave it to my dad and asked him to check it out for me."

"So you told your father about the possibility of Annie being followed?"

"Yes. It isn't much—I mean, the lady may not have been following her at all."

Rocky pulled his hand back and nodded. "Good. It may be nothing, but it's worth looking into."

He turned to Mrs. Phillips. "Do you remember seeing a vehicle like the one Jennie described around here?"

"I'm afraid not."

"There's something else." Jennie licked her lips. Rocky's penetrating gaze always made her feel nervous. "She mentioned seeing a teal blue van a lot. We saw one Thursday on the way to the meet." She explained what had happened. "That van turned out to be Debra Noble's."

"The woman on the 22 News?" Rocky gave her a patronizing smile. "You're saying Debra Noble was following you?"

"No. She was at Trinity for the meet. She interviewed some of the kids." Jennie frowned. "Raked my dad over the coals because he was watching me instead of tracking down that serial killer."

"Ah yes, I heard about that."

"You can't blame him for getting upset with her."

"Listen, if it had been me, I doubt I'd have handled it with that much diplomacy." He glanced down at his notes. "This van—what was your point?"

"I just mentioned it because . . . well, even though Debra wasn't following Annie, someone else with that color van could have been."

Rocky shifted his gaze to Mrs. Phillips. "Do you remember seeing either of the vehicles Jennie described around here?"

"No. But I'm often not here when Annie gets home from school. I work part time at The Book End. It's a new and used store downtown. . . ." Her voice faded.

"I'd like that list now, ma'am."

Mrs. Phillips handed it to him. Rocky passed it to Jennie and Lisa. "Can you girls think of anyone I should add?"

They couldn't.

"I'll be going, then." Rocky pushed back his chair and gave Mrs. Phillips a business card. "Give me a call if you hear anything. With any luck at all, your daughter will come home on her own. She may have decided to spend the night at a friend's house."

"I hope so. I've called most of her closest friends. They haven't seen her. I just wish there were something more I could do."

"I suggest you stay here in case she comes back. There's a good chance she will, but we'll continue to canvass the neighborhood and let the rest of the departments know she's missing."

The moment he stepped outside, Jennie and Lisa stood. "We need to be going, too, Mrs. Phillips," Jennie said. "We just wanted to let you know that we're going to try to find Annie."

"Jeanette, do you want me to—" A woman with silver white hair came down the wide, circular stairs. "Oh, I'm sorry. I didn't realize anyone else was here."

"Mother, these are Annie's friends—Jennie McGrady and Lisa Calhoun. Girls, this is my mother, Nora Ellison."

The girls greeted the older woman, glad Annie's mother had someone to be with her during her ordeal. The name Ellison sounded familiar, but Jennie couldn't place it. Heading back to the car, Jennie waved at Rocky, who was sitting in his patrol car and talking on his radio.

He leaned out the window and motioned for her to come over. "Go ahead and get in my car," Jennie said to Lisa. "He probably wants to lecture me about being careful."

"Or maybe he wants to ask you out."

Jennie rolled her eyes. "Get real, Lisa. He's old enough to be my . . . older brother."

Jennie sighed as she approached the driver's side of Rocky's vehicle. "Okay, I'm ready."

"Really?" He raised an eyebrow in a teasing manner. "For what?"

She folded her arms. "For you to tell me to mind my own business."

He tossed her that killer smile of his. "I don't need to do that anymore. At least I hope not. I wanted to thank you for the information and get your take on this business with Annie. Do you think she ran off, or do you really think she may be in danger?"

Jennie suppressed a wide grin. She loved it when adults took her seriously. She just wished she could give him an intelligent response. "I wish I knew. I wouldn't have pegged Annie as the type to run away. On the other hand, hearing that you were adopted and that your real mom threw you away . . . If that happened to me, I might run away too."

"Somehow I doubt that. What about the woman you thought was following her?"

"I'm sure she was. I caught a glimpse of her face in the rearview mirror at a stoplight and had the feeling she might have recognized me. She was wearing sunglasses, but still . . ." Jennie bit her lip. "I think we scared her off."

"I'll check it out. In the meantime, try to stay out of trouble."

Jennie smiled. "I thought you weren't going to lecture me."

"Couldn't resist."

Jennie caught her lower lip between her teeth again. "Did Mrs. Phillips tell you about the article in the school paper that got Annie so upset?"

"Yeah—tough way to learn you're adopted."

"Everyone's blaming Gavin Winslow for writing that article, but he didn't do it."

"Right now I'm not too concerned with who wrote it, but I am worried about Annie's reaction and her whereabouts. If she did run away—or even if she was abducted—there's not much chance of finding her. Speaking of which, I'm surprised you haven't been out looking for her."

"I figure we can help more by finding out who wrote the article. There might be a connection. Maybe the person who wrote it is the same one who's been following her. It's possible that same person abducted her—I mean, if that's what happened. On the other hand, it could be a nasty prank."

"If you come up with any answers, let me know."

Jennie backed away from the car and promised to call him if she uncovered any new information. He didn't seem at all interested in Gavin's possible guilt or innocence. His primary concern was finding Annie. Hers was, too, but she planned to go about it in a different way.

Clackamas Town Center was packed with its usual crowd of Saturday shoppers and mall walkers. Jennie and Lisa hurried to the food court. Gavin was waiting alone at one of the tables that overlooked the ice-skating rink.

"Hi." Jennie sank onto the plastic seat. "What happened to Allison and B.J.?"

"They couldn't come." He made a face. "Mr. Beaumont is afraid someone is targeting Allison again."

"Because of what happened to Annie?" Lisa asked.

"I guess I can see why he'd be worried," Jennie said. "They almost lost her the last time."

"That's true," Lisa added, "but anyone can see that Annie is the real target here."

"What makes you say that?" Gavin rested his elbows on the table and leaned forward. "The article pretty much trashed everyone. Annie just took it harder than anyone else."

Jennie told him about Annie's suspicions of being followed and about the discussion they'd had with Annie's mother and Rocky.

"So she came back and left again?" Gavin asked.

"That's what has me worried," Jennie went on. "According to Annie's mom, she was with Shawn last night. He dropped her off around eleven, but she didn't go inside. I'd like to talk to Shawn—find out exactly what happened. Something about this doesn't sound right. Shawn may be lying about dropping her off."

"I don't think Shawn would do that," Lisa said. "He's a sweet guy and really cares about Annie."

"Could she have asked him to drop her off somewhere and not tell her parents?"

Lisa's forehead wrinkled in a frown. "He might. But I don't think he'd let Annie's parents worry like that, do you?"

"I guess there's only one way to find out." Jennie drew a pad and pen out of her backpack and wrote, *Contact Shawn.*

"Good luck," Gavin said. "If he's gone camping, he probably won't be back in town until tomorrow night."

"You may be right." She circled the words she'd written. "So we work with what we have." On a new sheet of paper she began listing the events so far.

*Annie thinks someone may be stalking her. (Suspect may be driving a teal van or beige Cadillac.)*

*Someone breaks into journalism room—edits Gavin's article.*

*Annie finds out she's adopted. Runs away from home or was taken.*

"Annie said she hadn't gotten any threats or hate mail." Jennie tapped her pen on the table. "This article may be a form of that."

"With my name on it." Gavin groaned. "I'm dead."

"I wonder why they used your name." Jennie opened her bag and pulled out her wallet. The food smells were getting to her, and she hadn't had time to eat lunch yet.

"I wrote the original article. My by-line was already there, but everything I said about them was positive. I wanted all the girls to have an equal chance. The article was all ready to go Thursday afternoon. Someone came in during the night and rewrote it."

"I don't understand why you didn't catch it before it went out. Tell me about the paper. How was it possible for someone to change your article?"

"It's all laid out in the computer. Mrs. Andrews and I had already edited it—all except the last page, where I planned to put the information about the swim meet and put it to bed."

"Wait a minute." Lisa raised an eyebrow. "What do you mean, 'put it to bed'?"

"It's newspaper slang. Means it's ready to go. Once I finished the article, I checked the spacing on that page, and it was supposed to be all set. Then all we have to do when we come in on Friday is run it off, fold it, and give it to Mrs. Talbot to distribute to the students." He sighed and slouched down in the chair, stretching his long legs out in front of him. "I didn't know about the article until school was out on Friday and people started reading it."

"So who rewrote it and why?" Jennie mused. "How did they get in to the journalism room? And when?"

# 7

"First," Jennie said before Gavin and Lisa could answer, "I need some brain food." Jennie stood up. "I'm going to get an energy juice drink. You guys want anything?"

"A lemonade," Lisa requested.

"I'm fine." Gavin took a sip of whatever he was drinking. "Just hurry. We need to get to the bottom of this."

Jennie got a tropical energy booster drink and a pink lemonade, grabbed a couple of straws and napkins, then made her way back to the table.

"Have you figured out who did it yet?" She settled back into the chair and handed Lisa her drink. "What?" she asked when neither Gavin nor Lisa answered.

"Um . . . nothing." Lisa cleared her throat. She looked embarrassed.

"Am I interrupting something? If I am, I can go away for a while."

"No," Gavin said a little too quickly. "We were just talking. I told Lisa I hoped she was elected Fall Festival Queen."

"Hmm." Jennie had never figured Lisa might be interested in Gavin romantically. Lisa usually went for the more muscular type. Gavin's sudden interest in her cousin surprised Jennie. No reason why it should. A lot of guys liked Lisa. She was so cute and bubbly and had a fantastic figure. Jennie, however, was built more like a telephone pole. *Don't go there, McGrady,* she reminded herself. She was learning to live with the personality, shape, and gifts that were unique to her and not wish she were like Lisa or anyone else.

Besides, over the summer she'd had her share of admirers.

Lisa smiled. "Thank you, Gavin. That's sweet. Problem is, if I do win, I'm going to need an escort. Right now I'm not going with anybody." Her green eyes twinkled. "I suppose you're taking B.J.?"

Gavin blushed. "Where did you get that idea?"

"Well, you two have been spending a lot of time together. I just thought . . ."

"I've been giving her photography lessons. I think Russ asked her. But if you want, I could take you."

"Well, thanks a heap, friend," Jennie teased. "I was hoping you'd go with me."

"You were?" Gavin pushed his glasses back.

"I'm kidding." Jennie took a sip of her drink. "I'll just go by myself. Or I may not go at all."

"You could ask Ryan," Lisa suggested.

"Right." Jennie had to admit the idea appealed to her, but he might still be seeing Camilla. She wouldn't ask—it would hurt too much if he turned her down.

"What about that guy from Oregon State?" Gavin asked.

"Scott Chambers," Lisa added. "Why don't you ask him, Jennie? He really likes you."

"He likes his environmental causes more. I doubt he'd have the time. Last time he called me, he was all excited about going to Iceland to work with Keiko."

Lisa gave her an accusing look. "Why didn't you tell me?"

Jennie shrugged. "What did you want me to say? 'Oh, by the way, I've been dumped for a whale'?"

"Gavin could take both of us." Lisa brushed back her hair.

"Both—?" Gavin squeaked.

"Why not?" Lisa chuckled. "We're all good friends."

"Sounds okay to me." Jennie nodded. From the silly grin on Gavin's face, Lisa had boosted his ego into another galaxy. That was good. Gavin hadn't been very happy since his girlfriend, Courtney, moved back to New York with her dad. He was smart, cute, and available, but the girls weren't exactly breaking down walls to go out with him.

"Now that we've settled that," Jennie said, "let's get back to business." She told Gavin her theories about how someone may have gotten into the journalism room. He agreed, then went through the list of people who contributed to the paper and might have had access.

"It's a long list." Lisa tossed her empty drink container in a nearby trash can.

"Too long," Gavin said, "but I suppose we should get started."

"Seems like a waste of time." Lisa crumpled a damp napkin. "There's no reason for any of the journalism students to print garbage like this."

"Maybe." Jennie toyed with her straw and focused on the moisture dripping down the side of the paper cup. "But the fact remains that someone did it. This person is vindictive, knows how the paper goes together, and had to have done some extensive research. The only motive here that I can see is to hurt Annie."

"And hurt her chances of being elected Fall Festival Queen," Gavin added.

"Which is why I keep going back to the other contestants. We know Lisa didn't do it. What about B.J.? I'd hate to think of her as the kind of person who would write something like this, but . . ."

Gavin sighed. "I've wondered about that myself. She'd like Allison to win, but not that much. She's changed a lot since she came to live with the Beaumonts. Seems more settled and happy. She enjoys working on the paper." He shook his head. "It doesn't fit."

"My thoughts exactly," Lisa agreed. "It has to be someone on the outside."

"Lisa, I know how hard it is for you to see any of the kids being this cruel, but face it—who else would even care?" Jennie turned to watch the skaters on the ice below. Speculating was getting them nowhere. "I still think the key to all of this has to do with whoever has been following Annie. We just have to figure out who that is."

After a long silence Jennie said, "Sitting here isn't going to get us anywhere. I'm going to call Mom—see if she's talked to Dad yet. If she hasn't heard from him, I'm going back to Annie's place—see if the police have had any luck. I want to know who was driving that beige car."

Gavin threw away his cup. "Can you drop me off at *The Oregonian*? I'm going to write an article about the break-in. Then I'm going to call everybody connected with the school paper." *The Oregonian* was the Portland area's primary newspaper, and Gavin worked there part time as a reporter.

"I could talk to some of Annie's friends," Lisa volunteered. "She might be staying with someone and have sworn them to secrecy."

"Good idea." Jennie cleared the table, slipped the strap of her backpack over her shoulders, and headed for the pay phones.

---

"Any luck?" Lisa asked when Jennie joined her and Gavin at the exit.

"Waste of thirty-five cents." Jennie frowned. "Dad hadn't called, and I woke Mom up from a nap."

"I appreciate the ride." Gavin opened the passenger door and climbed into the backseat. "Takes me too long to get around on my bike."

"When are you getting your driver's license?" Jennie asked, pretending annoyance at having to drive him. She really didn't mind—especially when she was able to drive him home or pick him up. Gavin lived on a farm in East County. She loved the country setting. She also enjoyed talking with his mom, Maddie, who was a writer.

He shrugged. "I don't have a car and can't afford the insurance, so what's the use? Unlike you two, who are spoiled rotten and have your parents subsidizing you, I have to pay for everything. Trust me—it's expensive. I'd rather save the money I make for college. Besides, if I had my own car, I wouldn't have an excuse to ride with two beautiful women."

"Yeah, right," Jennie grumped. "I saw the photo of me you put in the school paper. I'd hardly call that beautiful. Thanks a bunch."

"Hey—it was a good action shot. Anyway, it isn't the photo; it's the numbers people will be looking at."

Lisa slid into the seat beside her and pulled the seat belt around. "Numbers, huh? Like 30–23–30?"

"Lisa!" Jennie huffed.

Lisa laughed. "Relax, Jen. I was only kidding. You are so uptight."

"Well, I don't think you need to let the world know my measurements."

"I'm sure Gavin won't tell anyone."

Gavin leaned forward. "You want to run that by me again, Lisa? I'll put it in next week's edition."

"That is not funny." Jennie started the car and backed out of her parking space as she heard the click of Gavin's seat belt.

"Sick—that's what you two are. Just plain sick." Jennie caught Gavin's wide grin in the rearview mirror and tossed one back at him.

———

After dropping Gavin off at the newspaper office and promising to pick him up later, Jennie and Lisa continued on to Jennie's house, where Lisa had left her car that morning. She didn't come in, saying she was going to pay a visit to Allison and B.J., then to Charity Brooks and some of the other girls Annie ran around with.

It was only after Lisa was gone that Jennie remembered what Annie had said about Charity when they were driving to the pool on Thursday. *"I wouldn't be surprised if it was Charity,"* Annie had said. *"She hates me. I'm not sure why."*

Jennie crept into the house in case her mother was still taking a nap. She hurried into the kitchen, grabbed an apple, checked the answering machine and message pad beside the phone, then went upstairs to her room.

There she tried to call her father, but he was still out on a case. Rocky wasn't available either. Frustrated, she finished her apple and wrote her mom a note saying she was going back over to Annie's.

At three-thirty she drove up to the curb in front of Annie's house and parked behind a patrol car. Three cars filled the driveway—one of them was Debra Noble's teal blue minivan.

# 8

"Well, hi, Jennie." Debra was just getting out of her van and glanced back toward the street. "What are you doing here?"

"I was about to ask you the same thing. I'm a friend of Annie's. Do you know if they've found her?"

"I'm afraid not. I heard about her disappearance and decided to interview the family. We'll do a segment on the six o'clock news and again at eleven." She glanced toward the house. "Excuse me, but I should get inside. Are you going in?"

"I was. M-maybe I shouldn't."

"You said you were Annie's friend?"

"Uh-huh. She goes to my school." Jennie realized after she'd said it that Debra already knew that.

"Jennie, why don't you stay? It might be good to interview a classmate."

"Um . . . I'm not sure I want to do that."

"Don't worry. I won't ask any 'stupid' questions." She gave Jennie a broad smile that said she'd forgiven Jennie for the comment she'd made after the meet. "I just want to do what I can to help the police find her—or convince her to come home."

"I do too." Jennie told her about Annie's concern that someone may have been stalking her.

A frown set on Debra's clear features. "That's what my police informant said. I hope that's not the case.

"Oh, here's Les."

Jennie looked back at the Channel 22 News van. The cameraman slid out of the van and opened the back to pull out his equipment. The three of them walked in together.

Rocky and Annie's father stood off to her right, just inside a room that looked like an office. Except for Rocky's fleeting glance in her direction, the two men ignored her.

Jennie walked past without acknowledging him. While they were making introductions and setting up, Jennie sat on the stairway in the entry, watching.

Dr. Phillips wore a polo shirt and shorts. His tan, muscular legs and arms bore evidence to the hours he spent outdoors—probably playing golf. She'd noticed a cart sitting just inside the open garage door, and from his bewildered look, she assumed he'd just come home.

"Is all of this really necessary?" Dr. Phillips said. "Annie's upset. Give her a little time to cool off, and she'll be back."

"You seem certain of that," Rocky said.

"I am. I know my daughter. Jeanette tends to blow things out of proportion. She shouldn't have called you or the media into this. It's a family affair." He shook his head. "Annie's going to be even more upset when she hears we've brought in the police and reporters. And I don't think the media attention is going to help at all. I told my wife not to worry this morning before I left."

"Dr. Phillips, there's reason to believe your daughter may have been abducted."

"What? That's impossible. I mean . . ."

Rocky related the discussion he, Jennie, and Mrs. Phillips had had earlier. Jennie found it odd that Mrs. Phillips hadn't told her husband, but maybe she hadn't had a chance. What she found even harder to accept was the fact that his daughter hadn't come home all night and he'd gone out golfing.

"We're ready to start." Debra spoke briefly to the two men and ushered them closer to the camera. She placed Dr. and Mrs. Phillips together on the couch, with Jennie next to them. Rocky was to stand next to Debra.

"Okay, Les. Whenever you're ready."

Les responded by turning on the camera. "Go ahead."

"Good evening, I'm Debra Noble." Debra spoke into the microphone and looked directly at the camera. "Many of you will remember Annie Phillips as the perky young lady from Trinity

High School whom I interviewed just last week. Annie was one of four girls hoping to gain the title of Trinity's Fall Festival Queen. Today Annie is in the news again, only on a much sadder note. Annie left her home last evening at eight-thirty and has not returned. Her boyfriend, Shawn Conners, allegedly dropped her off around eleven, but her mother told police this morning that Annie is still missing.

"We're here this afternoon at Annie's home with her parents, Dr. Paul Phillips and his wife, Jeanette. Annie's good friend Jennie McGrady is here, as well, along with Officer Dean Rockwell from the Portland police.

"Officer Rockwell, I understand you're heading up the investigation into Annie Phillips's disappearance." Debra stuck the microphone in Rocky's face.

He leaned away from it. "At this point everything is speculation. We're checking into several leads."

"Do you think she was abducted?"

"We're not ruling out that possibility. Right now we're looking for information. If anyone knows anything about Annie Phillips's whereabouts, I urge them to call the police immediately."

"Thank you, Officer Rockwell." Debra turned away from him and moved to an empty chair near the Phillipses and sat down. "Dr. and Mrs. Phillips, I know this is a difficult time for you. I understand that Annie became upset when she discovered she was adopted."

"Yes." Mrs. Phillips dabbed at her eyes with a tissue. "We should have told her before. I see that now. I just wish we knew what's happened to her. We love her so much."

"I'm sure you do." Debra went on to tell about the story that had appeared in the school paper and how it led to Annie discovering she had been a throw-away baby.

Debra then focused on Jennie, and the camera followed her lead. "Jennie, can you give us any insight as to what might have happened to Annie?"

"Not really. She told me at school a couple of days ago that she was being followed. That's what makes this so scary."

"It is frightening indeed." Going back to Mrs. Phillips, Debra said, "Annie is your only child, isn't she?"

"Yes. We were never able to have children of our own. Paul was on duty at the hospital the night Annie was found. We were thrilled when we were chosen to adopt her. She's been a delightful child. I just pray nothing's happened to . . ." Mrs. Phillips dissolved in sobs.

Her husband settled an arm around her. "May I say something?"

"Certainly." Debra tipped the mike toward him.

"Annie, honey, I know this is hurtful for you, but running away isn't going to solve anything. If you're watching, please know that we would never deliberately hurt you. Adopted or not, you're our daughter, and we love you more than life itself."

"Okay. That should do it," Debra said. "I'll do the wrap-up on the air. Thanks. We'll need a recent photo of Annie."

Mrs. Phillips stood. "I'll get one."

"Dr. Phillips, I'm curious. You were talking to your daughter as though she had run away. Apparently you don't agree with the abduction theory."

"No, I don't." He closed his eyes. "I can't."

"Well, I hope you're right." Debra placed the microphone in her large briefcase and took the framed 8 × 10 portrait of Annie that Mrs. Phillips handed her. "Thank you for doing the interview. Let's just hope it does some good. Have you talked with anyone else?"

"No," Dr. Phillips said. "And I don't think I can go through this again."

"You probably won't have to. Once I run the exclusive, the other stations will pick it up. The more attention this gets, the more likely we'll find someone who has seen her."

"If it doesn't alienate her completely," Dr. Phillips muttered.

Debra apparently didn't hear him. If she did, she didn't acknowledge it.

"I appreciate your staying," Debra told Rocky. "You will call me if anything breaks, won't you?"

"You'll be one of the first to know." He gave her a smile and walked out with her. If Debra hadn't been at least ten years older than he was, Jennie would have suspected him of flirting with the woman. Maybe he was. Age didn't matter to some people.

ABANDONED

Debra was definitely flirting with him—batting her baby blues and turning on the charm.

Jennie would have followed them outside, but Dr. Phillips stopped her. "Jennie, I understand we have you to thank for this abduction business." His expression and the harsh edge in his voice told her he wasn't thankful at all.

"Me?" Jennie automatically went on the defensive. "Annie told me she was being followed. I just told the police."

"Annie never mentioned anything like that to us."

"She was afraid to in case it wasn't for real. She didn't want anyone laughing at her."

He frowned. "If anyone is to blame in this, it's that young man who edits the paper."

"Gavin didn't—"

"Oh yes, Gavin Winslow. You can tell your friend for me that he'll be hearing from my attorney."

"But—"

"I'd like you to leave now, Miss McGrady. I need to talk with my wife and try to pull what's left of my family back together again."

Jennie clenched her fists and stepped outside. The door slammed behind her. "How rude." *But the man is hurting*, part of her reasoned. Anger, denial, it was all part of the grieving process. Jennie had been through it all years ago when government agents came to their house to tell them her father was missing and presumed dead. She'd been angry too. Still, Dr. Phillips had no right to lash out at her. She hadn't done anything but try to help.

The cameraman waved and pulled away from the curb. Rocky stood in the driveway next to the teal van talking to Debra through the open window.

"I'm sorry for the inconvenience," Rocky said.

"Not a problem. I'm just glad to see our men in blue doing their job." Debra settled a perfectly manicured hand on Rocky's. "Thanks."

Jennie hurried past them to her car and ducked inside.

"Jennie, hold on," she heard Rocky shout over the sound of her engine.

She heaved an exasperated sigh. Jennie wanted nothing more

53

than to get out of there and go home. She hadn't done anything wrong, but Dr. Phillips made her feel as though she was the one responsible for his daughter's disappearance. Now Rocky was probably going to lecture her too.

*You're not being fair, McGrady. He was nice enough before.* Maybe he had information on the license number.

Rocky stepped up to the car a moment later and pressed his palms against the roof. "I understand you were trying to get ahold of me earlier."

"I called to see if you'd gotten a name to go with the license number of the car that was following Annie."

"Yes, I did. Your dad gave me the information."

"And . . ."

"And nothing. You were wrong."

"Who was it?"

"I can't tell you that. The last thing that lady needs is for you to start harassing her and making accusations."

"Can't you just—"

"No. I don't want to get tough with you, Jennie, but rules are rules. Now, the best thing for you to do is butt out and let us handle things."

"I still think she was following Annie."

"You'll have to trust me on this one, Jen. You're way off base. Leave it alone."

Jennie swallowed hard and stared straight ahead. "Fine. I'm going home. And I still think the woman in the beige Caddy was following Annie."

"Look, you're a great kid, Jennie. You've got a caring heart and a good head on your shoulders. Everyone makes mistakes. Your biggest one right now is not being able to admit you were wrong. You gotta know when to cut your losses."

Jennie put the car into gear. "I'd better go. All I seem to be doing here is getting in the way."

"I'll talk to you later." Rocky stepped back from the car.

"Right." Jennie pulled away a little faster than necessary.

"I should have stayed home and worked on my report." She glanced at her tear-streaked face in the rearview mirror and brushed the moisture away with the back of her hand. She wasn't sure what had caused the tears—being yelled at by Dr. Phillips or having Rocky tell her she was wrong. Maybe it was because she hated being wrong.

Jennie turned into a small market, where she bought a large Coke. She was too upset to go home just yet. She wasn't really great about hiding her feelings. Mom seemed to know when anything was wrong. The last thing Jennie wanted to do at the moment was talk about it.

She took the long way home, stopping at the park near her home to walk along the trail by the lake and watch the swans and ducks. By four-thirty she'd worked out most of her anger and hurt and was driving into her driveway. She'd finally accepted the fact that Rocky had a point. She had no proof that the person in the beige Cadillac was following Annie. All she had was her imagination and intuition. Maybe she'd just wanted to believe that her intuition was foolproof.

There was another answer to Annie's claim that she was being followed. Maybe Annie just wanted attention. Suppose she found out about the adoption and wanted to get back at her parents. She could have written the column herself and run away. *Ridiculous.* Jennie reversed the direction her thoughts had taken and went inside. The house smelled like dinner. It was quiet.

Mom had left a note on the counter. *Gone to Kate's to pick up Nick and to take over Bernie's dog food and dishes. Dinner's ready. You can set the table. I'll be home by six.*

Jennie meandered over to the Crockpot, lifted the lid, and inhaled the wonderful aroma of beef stew. She quickly set the table, then went into the living room and stretched out on the couch. She lay there with her eyes closed for several minutes and felt herself drifting off. Part of her begged for a nap. Another urged her to get up and work on her project. "In a minute," she told the nagging voice. "Just let me rest. . . ."

A thud from the room above—her room—brought her fully awake. It took half a second for her brain to register the terrifying fact. She was not home alone.

# 9

She was halfway up the stairs before her common sense kicked in. *You don't confront burglars. You call the police.*

Jennie came to an abrupt halt. She started to make a hasty retreat when the toilet flushed. Jennie stood her ground. She doubted that a burglar would take the time to go to the bathroom and wash his or her hands. The door to the bathroom opened.

Jennie released the breath she'd been holding and bounced up the remaining steps. "Do you have any idea how many people are looking for you?"

"Jennie!" Annie stood in the middle of the hallway with her hand on her chest. "You scared me half to death."

"Good. Why are you here? How did you get in? The door was locked."

Annie ran a hand through her messed-up hair. She looked as though she'd been sleeping. "I . . . no, it wasn't. I saw that your car was gone but decided to try the door anyway. I thought everyone was gone. Then I saw that your mom was asleep on the couch. I went up to your room. I . . . I'm sorry, but I was so tired and needed a place to hang out."

"Where did you go after Shawn dropped you off last night?"

"How did you. . . ?"

"Never mind that. Just answer me." Jennie probably should have been a little more kind, but right now she was fighting mad.

"I . . . I stayed outside in the doll house I used to play in when I was a little girl. This morning I waited until Dad left to play golf; then I took off. Can you believe it? I don't come home all night, and he still has to tee off at seven. I rode the bus around for a while. We went by the park, and I realized I was close to your house. I thought maybe you . . . Please don't be mad. I went to your room to wait for you and fell asleep."

Jennie opened the door to her room. Her bed had been slept in all right. "The least you can do is make my bed."

Annie hurried past her, straightened the sheets, and picked the comforter off the floor, all the while apologizing.

"Annie, just shut up, okay? I can't believe you ran away. You have to call your parents."

"No." She snapped up, looking like someone had slapped her. "They lied to me, Jennie. Don't you understand? My life is over." She sank onto the bed and buried her face in her hands.

"Don't you think you're making too much of this? So you're adopted. Millions of kids are adopted. You've got parents who love you. There are kids out there who don't have anyone to take care of them." Jennie realized she was sounding like her mother, but at the moment she didn't care. Annie was acting like a spoiled brat.

"I thought you would understand."

Jennie sighed and went to sit beside her. She was having trouble sympathizing. In part, Jennie felt betrayed. "I'm trying. Look at it from my side. You have everything. You're rich and beautiful. You have a nice home and parents who love you. Besides, I just spent all day worrying that someone kidnapped you."

"Why would you think that?"

"Think about it. I was afraid that whoever had been following you might have abducted you. I told the police and your father what you'd said. They're both upset with me. Now I'll look like an idiot for sure—especially when they find out you're here."

Annie lifted her head. The long, sleepless night had left dark circles under her eyes. "I didn't mean to cause any trouble. Someone has been following me. And you even said—"

"Dead end. I had the police check the license number on that beige car we thought was your stalker. The police won't tell me who it is—they're afraid I'll harass her. The van you thought was after you belongs to Debra Noble. And she wasn't following you. Are you sure you're not making this up?"

"How can you say that? I thought you were my friend."

"Real friends are honest with each other."

"I *am* being honest. I'm not making anything up. I . . . I'm confused."

"I can see that. You need to talk to your mom and dad."

"They're not my—"

"Don't even say it." Jennie held up a hand to silence her. "They may not be your biological parents, and they may have made a mistake in not telling you about the adoption, but they *are* your parents. To be honest, I think telling a kid she'd been thrown away as a baby would be really hard to do. I don't blame them for putting it off." Jennie reached across Annie to the phone on the nightstand and handed her the receiver. "Call them."

Annie pushed the phone away. "I can't. Not yet."

"Then I will."

"No, please." She grabbed the phone away from Jennie. "I'll call. Just give me a few minutes to get used to the idea."

Jennie bounced off the bed and paced the floor.

"I don't want to get you into trouble, Jennie. Maybe I should leave."

"Don't worry about that. Maybe they'll be so happy to see you, they won't care where you were hiding out."

"I'll tell them you didn't know." She hung up the phone.

Jennie sighed. "I doubt they'll believe you." She picked up the phone again and punched in the number for information.

"Who are you calling?"

"Debra Noble." Jennie asked the operator for Channel 22.

"You can't be serious. I don't want her to know I ran away."

"It's too late for that. She not only knows; she interviewed your parents and me. If I don't call her to let her know you're okay, your picture will be on the six o'clock news." When the receptionist for the station answered, Jennie asked for Debra.

"Oh no. How could this have happened?" Annie moaned.

Jennie put a hand over the receiver. "You ran away from home. You told me someone was following you. Your mother called the police because she was worried about you. The entire church is praying for you. In an hour the entire state of Oregon and half of Washington will be looking for you."

"Debra isn't available at the moment. Would you like to leave a message on her voice mail?" the receptionist asked.

"Yes, thanks." Jennie waited through the voice mail message.

"Tell her not to run the interview," Annie begged.

Into the phone Jennie said, "Debra, this is Jennie McGrady. I thought you'd like to know Annie's okay. She doesn't want you to run the interview. Call me for details."

When Jennie hung up, Annie picked up the phone. "I guess I'd better call now, huh?"

"I think that's a good idea." Jennie offered up a quick prayer of thanks. "As soon as you're finished, I'll take you home."

"Where are you going?" Annie asked.

"Downstairs. Figured you'd like some privacy. I'll be in the kitchen. Let me know when you're ready to go."

Jennie wasn't all that worried about Annie's privacy. In truth, she'd have liked to stick around to hear what she had to say, but she wanted to use the other phone. She hurried to the phone in the kitchen and dialed Lisa's number. Aunt Kate answered.

"She isn't here, Jennie. I needed the car and dropped her off downtown. I thought you were supposed to pick her and Gavin up at *The Oregonian*."

"Whoops. I forgot. I'll go get them right away. Is Mom still there?"

"Yes, did you want to talk to her?"

"No, that's okay. Just tell her Annie's been found. She's on her way home."

"Thank goodness. We'll let the prayer chain know."

"Thanks, I'll see you later. Love you. Bye."

Jennie hung up and called the newspaper office, then waited for the receptionist to put her through to Gavin.

"Where's Gavin?" Jennie asked when Lisa came on the line.

"He's talking to one of the reporters."

"She's here."

"Who?"

"Annie."

"That's great. Is she okay?"

"Yeah. She's calling her parents on my phone upstairs. She was in my room when I came home. Can you believe it?"

"Well, I'm not surprised she'd come to you," Lisa said. "I'm glad she's safe. When are you picking us up? I thought you'd be here by now."

"Um . . . to be honest, I forgot." Jennie filled her in on the events of the afternoon. "Anyway, when I left the Phillipses' place I was pretty upset. Then I came home and found Annie. I'm taking her home, then swinging by to pick you up."

"Good. I think we have an idea who messed up Gavin's article."

"Really? Who?"

"I can't say for sure. That's what Gavin is talking to the reporter about. We'll tell you all about it when you pick us up."

"I can't wait. Talk to you later." Jennie hung up, grabbed a couple of Tootsie Pops from the container in the cupboard, and hurried back to the stairs. "Annie?"

No answer. A feeling of dread settled deep in Jennie's stomach. "She wouldn't."

Jennie hurried to her room. It was empty. Jennie had never thought of herself as a violent person, but at the moment she felt like strangling Annie Phillips.

"Annie?" Jennie called again. Still no answer.

"Fine," Jennie muttered. "Run away. See if I care."

She ran back downstairs. Maybe Annie was already outside. Even though the thought entered her head, she was surprised to see Annie sitting on the porch swing. Her frustration came out in a huge sigh. "I thought you'd run off again."

"I almost did." Annie looked so sad, Jennie's anger fizzled like a drowned fire.

"You did call your parents, didn't you?"

"Yes." Her wide blue eyes filled with tears. "They aren't mad at me. At least, that's what Mom says. Daddy is, I'm sure. Not because I ran away, but because of all the fuss."

"You're right about that. He already is mad—but not at you." Jennie thought about what he'd said to Rocky about knowing his daughter. *Guess he was right about that too.*

Twenty minutes later Jennie dropped Annie off at her house. Jennie opted not to go inside.

"I'll call you tonight and let you know how it goes," Annie

promised. "Don't worry. I'll tell Dad you didn't have anything to do with my decision."

Jennie waited until Annie went inside before driving away. She turned on the radio. Elton John was singing about a guy named Daniel leaving on a plane. Jennie wished she were going with him.

By the time she reached the newspaper office, Jennie felt better. Annie was home and safe. Gavin and Lisa may have already found the culprit who'd pulled that nasty prank. The big question remaining was the one regarding Annie's stalker. Now Jennie seriously wondered if there even was one.

Jennie pulled into a parking place and went inside. Gavin was sitting on the corner of one of the desks, talking to a woman in a white classic-style dress shirt and blue jeans. A tweed blazer hung on the back of her chair. Lisa stood to one side, listening in on their conversation.

"Hey, Jen—over here." Gavin waved at her. "I want to show you something."

Instead of introducing Jennie to the woman, he shoved a manila folder at her. "Check this out."

Jennie opened it and began to sift through newspaper clippings and articles. The one on top was yellowed—the caption read, "Baby Found in Dumpster." Jennie looked from Gavin to Lisa, then to the woman whose desk they surrounded. She looked familiar, but Jennie couldn't place her.

"This is research material for an article I was planning to write for next Sunday's paper," the woman said. "I've been planning to do a follow-up on throw-away babies to see how they are doing today. In order to do the article, I needed signed releases from all the people involved. I still have three families to go. Paul and Jeanette Phillips are on that list."

Jennie frowned. "You were going to write an article?"

"That's right. You can understand how shocked I was when Gavin showed me your school paper."

Jennie handed the file back to her. "So what are you trying to say? That someone got ahold of your file and—"

"Not just someone, Jennie. My own daughter."

The moment she said it, Jennie knew who the woman was. Everything clicked into place. "You're Mrs. Brooks," she said. "Charity's mom."

# 10

"Gavin." Shannon Brooks picked up the file and tapped it on the desk. "I can't even begin to tell you how sorry I am about all this. You can rest assured that Charity will be coming forth with a full apology to Annie Phillips and you and a retraction for the school paper. In fact, I'll make certain she writes a special letter of apology to everyone involved by Monday."

She stuffed the file folders into her briefcase. "I had no idea she'd do something so . . . so vindictive. I'll be talking to the principal and Mrs. Andrews as well. I know Charity deserves it, but I hope they don't suspend her from school."

"I guess that will depend on her," Lisa said. "This will be tough for her. Tell Charity . . . well, tell her I'll be around if she needs to talk."

"That's very sweet, Lisa. I'm afraid Charity won't be talking on the phone or going anywhere with friends for a while." She stood and slipped her arms into her jacket. "May I have a copy of your school paper, Gavin?"

"Sure." Gavin hurried off to his desk, retrieved a copy of *The Trinity Tidings*, and brought it back to Charity's mom.

"Thanks. And again, I'm sorry for all the trouble this has caused."

"I'm just glad it's settled." Gavin rested a hip against the desk. "I can see we're going to have to beef up security in the journalism room. I'd still like to know how she got in."

"I'll find out." She gave them each a tight smile. "I must say, you are all taking this much better than I am." Shannon Brooks's white tennis shoes squeaked as she walked across the floor toward the entrance.

"Nice job, you two." Jennie gave them both a high five. "How did you make the connection?"

"It wasn't hard." Gavin led them back to his desk. "I over-heard Mrs. Brooks talking to someone on the phone about doing an article about throw-away babies." He shrugged. "So I asked her about it and showed her the article in *The Tidings*. I told her someone from school had written it, and she knew right away it was Charity."

"Has Charity confirmed it?" Jennie asked.

"It's obvious, isn't it?" Lisa asked.

"I suppose."

"Jennie McGrady, you are just jealous that Gavin and I cracked the case before you could."

"I am not."

"Are too."

Jennie rolled her eyes. "I am *not* jealous."

"Hey, no fighting, you two. Jennie's right. There is a slight chance that Charity is innocent. Very slight. I mean, what are the odds of someone else coming up with information like that about Annie at the same time?"

"Guess we'll know for sure on Monday." Jennie tossed her keys in the air and caught them. "You two ready to go?"

"Yep. Just let me close this down." Gavin dropped into his chair, wheeled over to the computer, and attacked the keyboard. Seconds later the program shut down and the computer screen went black. He collected his pack and gave them both a wide, satisfied grin. "Let's go."

"I feel sorry for Charity." Lisa pulled the seat belt across her lap and shoulders.

"Why?" Gavin settled himself into the backseat.

"It must be awful to feel that insecure about yourself that you feel like you have to tear your opponents down in order to win."

"You're saying Charity has low self-esteem?" Jennie adjusted the rearview mirror, then eased into the street.

"She must have. Maybe it's because her GPA isn't all that great. She really has to work hard to even pull Cs."

"You could be right. But what Charity did hurt more people than just Annie. She hurt Gavin, Allison, you, and Annie's parents. In fact, she hurt the entire school and cost the police bureau a lot of money."

"It's a ripple effect," Gavin said. "You throw a rock in a pond and it makes ripples. It affects everything in the pond. Charity threw a big rock, and Annie's life will never be the same. Neither will Charity's."

Lisa twisted around in her seat to look at him. "That's neat, Gavin. You should write an opinion piece for *The Tidings*. Maybe *The Oregonian* would print it too. About the trouble we cause when we make the wrong choices."

"Maybe I will."

"It started way before Charity, though," Jennie said. "Annie's birth mother threw the biggest rock of all when she decided to put her baby in that trash bin."

Saturday traffic was heavy on the I-84 and I-205 freeways. The worst, though, was at the Sunnyside exit, where cars were bumper-to-bumper.

While she drove, Jennie filled them in on her television experience, her run-in with Rocky, and coming home to find Annie in her house.

"Oh no." Jennie hit her forehead with the heel of her hand when she spotted the flashing lights of a patrol car on the side of the road.

"What's the matter?" Lisa turned to look as they passed the patrol car and a red sports car he'd stopped. "He's not after you."

"I know, but seeing the police car reminded me—I forgot to call Rocky to let him know about Annie. Now he's really going to be mad at me."

"I wouldn't worry about it, Jennie." Gavin leaned forward and rested his arms against the back of Lisa's seat. "I'm sure he knows by now."

An uneasy feeling grumbled in her stomach. She couldn't decide if she was nervous or scared. One thing for certain, she did not relish the prospect of seeing Rocky again anytime soon. "I'm sure he does."

Jennie glanced at her watch as she pulled into Gavin's driveway. "It's after six. I hope Debra got my message about not airing the interview she did with the Phillipses."

"You want to come in and find out? I'm sure my folks are watching the news."

"Better not," Jennie said. "I'm already late for dinner."

"Okay, see you later." He put a hand on each of their shoulders before getting out of the car. "Thanks for your help today."

"No problem," Jennie said.

"Call me later, okay?" Lisa called after him.

He paused on the porch and waved, his smile as wide as Texas. "I will."

Jennie turned to Lisa. "Since we're closer to my house, you want to eat with us? Our moms won't mind. I can take you home after dinner."

---

The next morning Lisa was still there. They'd gone to Lisa's house, but only to collect her things for an overnight stay. They were to meet Lisa's family at church, then spend the day together. Dad had one of his rare days off. Jennie still hadn't finished her project and prayed she'd find time to work on it during the week.

"Hey, girls," Dad called from the entry. "Get the lead out or we'll have to leave without you."

"Coming." Jennie practically fell down the stairs trying to get her shoes on while she walked. She stopped on the landing and slipped her feet into the low-heeled dress shoes.

"C'mon, Jennie." Nick knelt down beside her. "Dad says get the lead out. He's getting exaggerated."

Jennie chuckled. Nick was so cute when he imitated adults and got his words mixed up. "You mean exasperated."

"Yeah—that's what I said."

"I'm almost ready." Jennie ruffled his dark hair. "You want to take my bag out to the car?"

"Sure." He hoisted the heavy bag onto his shoulder. Though she was wearing a dress to church, she'd brought jeans and a T-shirt and sneakers to change into later. The bag also contained her Bible and a small notebook.

"I got lots of muscles. See?" He grunted under the strain.

"Hey, big guy. That's quite a load." Dad took the bag from him and tossed it in the trunk of the Oldsmobile. "Jennie, did you lock the door?"

"Yep." Jennie slipped on her sweater, then climbed into the backseat with Nick and Lisa and closed the door.

Nick promptly reached for his children's Bible and asked Jennie to read the story of David and Goliath to him.

Jennie read part of it, then turned the task over to Lisa. While Lisa read, Jennie watched her parents. It felt good to see them getting along. Before Dad had disappeared, it seemed like they were always fighting. Mom hated his being gone so much. Now they seemed more than willing to work things out.

At the moment, though, Dad looked grim, and Jennie suspected he was thinking about the serial killer he had yet to find.

"Would you like to talk about it?" Mom said.

He glanced over at her. "Not really. I'm trying to leave it behind today. I owe my family that much."

Mom reached over and squeezed his hand. "Thank you."

"For what?"

"Taking time out for us like this."

He grinned and kissed the back of her hand. "When a McGrady makes a promise . . ."

"He *usually* keeps it." Mom glanced back at Jennie. "Did you talk to Annie last night?"

"Yeah. She says she's okay with things now."

"Good. I'm glad she went home. They need to work things out as a family."

"I wish I could solve this case that easily," Dad said. "It's got me baffled. This last murder—it's like the others but it's not."

"You think it's a copycat killing?" Mom asked.

Dad nodded and gave her wan smile. "That's exactly what I think. I'm having a tough time coming up with a motive. The latest victim was a nurse—well liked. Not married. She seemed not to have an enemy in the world." He sighed heavily. "Yet somehow I don't get the impression that it was done by the same killer. Not the way—" He stopped and caught Jennie's intent gaze in the rearview mirror. "Why don't we talk about something else. I think the best thing for me and the investigation right now is to distance myself from it."

Jennie wanted to object but figured it wouldn't do much good.

"We could talk about names for the baby," Mom suggested.

Dad chuckled. "How about Alphonse if it's a boy?"

"Dad!" Jennie tipped her head back. "Tell me you're joking, please."

"I'll have you know Alphonse is a great German name."

"Right. It reminds me of Algernon."

"Now, Jennie," Dad said in a patronizing tone. "Algie is a very nice young man."

Algie was a friend. "He's nice, but I'd hate to have to live with a name like that. He told me that when he was little, kids used to call him Pond Scum."

"How about Noah or Isaiah?" Mom suggested. "I think I'd like something biblical."

"I know, I know." Nick waved his arm like he'd been taught in kindergarten. "We could call him Zaccheus. It would be a good name 'cause he would be a wee little man and I could sing it to him." Nick had determined they'd have a boy. Jennie was hoping for a girl. Mom and Dad just wanted a healthy baby.

They spent the next few minutes tossing names back and forth. Most of Dad's and Nick's were weird, but they had a few good laughs. They arrived at church and piled out of the car. Since their church building had burned down along with the school, Trinity now held services in the school gymnasium. About three hundred folding chairs sat in rows behind a make-shift stage and pulpit, and nearly all of them were full.

A small band of musicians to the right of the platform were tuning up and checking for sound. Music was Jennie's favorite part of the service. She enjoyed singing the eclectic assortment of praise songs and hymns.

Uncle Kevin, Aunt Kate, and Kurt were already seated. Lisa and Jennie filed into the same row with Jennie's parents and Nick.

The music started just after they'd arranged themselves.

They stood with the others, and soon Jennie forgot about her surroundings and focused on the words of the song. "Forget about yourselves and worship Him, Jesus Christ, the Lord."

After the service small groups clustered about. Jennie looked around for some of the other kids while Lisa headed for the rest room. Annie and her parents hadn't come, and Jennie couldn't blame them. It would be hard to face people after what had happened.

Charity and her mother were there, which surprised Jennie. Charity looked anything but happy. Jennie approached the duo with caution. "Hi, Charity, Mrs. Brooks."

"Hi, Jennie." Mrs. Brooks placed a restraining arm around Charity's shoulder. At her mother's urging, Charity muttered a hello.

"I . . . um . . ." Jennie wasn't sure what to say.

Charity took a deep breath. "Look, I'm sorry about trashing Annie in the paper, okay?"

"So you did do it?"

Charity's gaze wandered to the ground. "I didn't think it was a big deal. Politicians are always digging up their opponent's past and releasing it to the press."

"That doesn't make it right," Jennie and Mrs. Brooks said in unison. Jennie bit her lip. Good grief. She was sounding more and more like an adult these days.

"Look, I said I was sorry." Charity tucked her long, gleaming blond curls behind her ears. Her blue gaze lingered a moment on Jennie as if accusing her, then shifted to her mother. "Can we go now?"

"Charity, I'm curious," Jennie said. "How did you get into the journalism room?"

"That was the easiest part." She tossed Jennie a proud smile. "I took journalism last year and remembered that Mrs. Andrews kept an extra set of keys in her desk. I just took them, had a key made, and put them back."

Charity stepped back. "Mom, let's go. I need to get home if I'm going to write all those stupid letters and get my homework done."

Mrs. Brooks hesitated a moment, then told Jennie good-bye.

Charity lifted her chin and walked away.

Jennie watched them go. Charity didn't look all that repentant. She looked more like a kid caught in a lie, forced to come clean. She hated to think anyone would hurt someone the way Charity had hurt Annie and not feel truly sorry. All the apologies in the world would be for nothing if she didn't mean it. On the other hand, maybe Charity was just acting rude to cover up for her embarrassment.

Jennie moved on to talk with Gavin, Lisa, B.J., Allison, and Allison's boyfriend, Jerry.

Gavin hung an arm on Jennie's shoulder. "Hey, I noticed you were talking to Charity. I wanted to go over, too, but Lisa said I shouldn't."

"Probably a good idea. She wasn't in the greatest mood." Jennie told them about their conversation.

"That's too bad," Allison said. "We'll have to be sure to pray for her."

Jerry squeezed Allison's hand. He was the president of their church's youth group. A nice guy whose look never changed. Living on a working ranch, he was a real cowboy and never went anywhere without his jeans, boots, and hat. "I'll call the other kids and tell them too. She must really be hurting right now."

Jennie didn't feel all that sorry for Charity but didn't voice her opinion.

"Has anyone heard from Annie since she got home?" Allison asked.

Jennie told them she'd talked to her and related the message that Annie seemed to be coming around. The six of them moved outside of the building and stood on the front steps soaking in the sunshine. The cool October morning was turning into a warm Indian-summer day. Jennie removed her white knit sweater and folded it over her arm.

"Do you think someone is really following her, Jennie?" B.J. tapped her rolled-up Sunday school papers and church bulletin against her palm, her hazel eyes issuing their usual challenge. "I'd have checked it out myself, but Dad went ballistic when he heard Al and me talking about it."

"So far we've hit a couple of dead ends." Jennie shrugged and told her about the woman they'd seen following Annie on Friday, then sighed. "But the car belongs to some lady, and the police won't tell me who. Maybe she wasn't following Annie, but I'd sure like to talk to her."

"I bet I could find out for you, Jennie," Gavin said. "My uncle Ted works at the DMV. Do you still have the license number?"

Jennie flushed, embarrassed that she hadn't memorized it. "No, unless Lisa can remember it."

"I wrote it down and handed it to Jennie." Her green gaze brightened. "But I should be able to find the note pad. I haven't used it since, and I could do that thing—you know, where you rub a pencil across the indentation."

"Great!" Jennie grinned and gave her cousin's shoulders a squeeze. "See if you can find it and call me as soon as you get home."

"That may be a while. Don't forget, we're going to the Harvest Festival."

"Oh, right."

"We'd better go. Dad's already in the car." Allison stepped out of the circle. "Come on, B.J." She turned to Jerry and kissed his cheek. "Call me later."

"See you tomorrow," B.J. said. "Call me if you need help finding Annie's stalker."

"If there is one," Jennie said. "It was probably just Charity spying on her."

When they'd gone, Gavin got the signal from his folks and left as well. Jennie and Lisa spotted their parents in the crowd of adults gathered around the coffee and dessert tables just outside the sanctuary.

Jennie's mom and dad were talking to Annie's grandmother, Mrs. Ellison. A tall, attractive man with graying hair came up beside them. Shaking Dad's hand, he said, "Nice to see you again, Jason." He bestowed a friendly smile on Mom. "How's my favorite patient?"

Jennie eased in beside her dad. So that's where she'd heard Ellison's name. He was Mom's doctor.

Mom blushed. "I bet you say that to all your patients."

He chuckled, then looked at Jennie. "And this must be your daughter. Jennie, is that right?"

"Jennie is a friend of Annie's, darling," Mrs. Ellison said. "She's the one who brought Annie home."

"Oh yes." His gaze fastened on hers. "I heard my son-in-law was less than kind. I hope you'll forgive him. He and Jeanette have both been through a lot the last few days."

"No problem," Jennie said. "I didn't know you went to church here."

"We come occasionally with Paul and Jeanette," Mrs. Ellison said. "But we're thinking of becoming members. It's a good church."

"Jason," Dr. Ellison said, "I understand you've been working on that triple murder investigation. Terrible thing. Any leads?"

"Not much. But don't worry, we'll nail him."

"I hope so. Those of us who are pro-life advocates are getting nervous. Are you certain it's a man?"

"Not entirely. We're keeping our options open."

"Good. That's good. I'm sure with you working on the case, we have nothing to worry about."

The Ellisons said their good-byes and left. Moments later Aunt Kate and Uncle Kevin joined them, and the adults discussed where they would meet once they got to the festival grounds in downtown Portland.

Jennie tuned them out, her attention riveted on a car pulling out of the parking lot.

A beige Cadillac merged with the other cars. The woman driving had blond curly hair and wore sunglasses. The same woman who'd been following Annie.

# 11

"Jennie, it's time to go." Dad settled a hand on her shoulder.

Jennie's gaze was still transfixed on the intersection where the car had turned and disappeared. She debated telling her father, then decided against it. By the time they got to their car, it would be long gone. Not that her father would have gone after it anyway. Rocky had told her in no uncertain terms that the driver of that particular car had not been following Annie. So who was she to disagree? She sighed and followed her parents.

"Where are we going?"

"Hello," he chuckled. "Earth to Jennie. We're going to caravan. We'll eat lunch at the festival."

The rest of the afternoon dragged on. Not that she didn't enjoy herself. Harvest Festival was great with all the rides, delicious food, and exhibits. But Jennie couldn't keep her mind off the beige Caddy. She hadn't spotted it soon enough to get a license number, but her interest in tracking the driver down increased tenfold. It seemed much more than a coincidence that the car would be driving near both Annie's church and the school.

Once they got home, Lisa would try to find the number and give it to Gavin. She had other ways of finding out as well. Of course, maybe they'd get lucky and Gavin would come up with a name. Jennie didn't want to harass the person. She just needed to satisfy her curiosity.

———

When the phone rang that night at eight-thirty, Jennie

snatched it up, expecting to hear Lisa's voice, or maybe Gavin's, with an answer. It was neither.

"Ryan," she squeaked. Clearing her throat, she managed a somewhat normal "How are you?" She wasn't sure whether to be happy or sad. Her heart cheered while her brain told her to approach with caution. *He broke up with you,* she reminded herself. *He's dating Camilla.*

"I'm doing great. How 'bout you?"

"Good." Jennie pictured him stretched out on a chair in his living room, brushing his blond hair away from his face.

"What's going on? Have you solved any more mysteries lately?"

"Not exactly. I've mostly been doing homework."

"I know the feeling." He hesitated, and Jennie imagined his sky-blue eyes and cute smile.

"Um . . . so why did you call? If it's to remind me about your birthday, I already got you a gift."

"You did? Cool." He sighed heavily. "But that isn't the reason I called."

"Oh." Jennie twisted her long, thick braid around her hand like a rope and tugged at it.

"How's Scott?"

"Who?" Jennie frowned at the unexpected question.

She could almost hear the relief in his voice when he said, "Your boyfriend. Scott Chambers."

"Oh, him. Okay, I guess. He's studying sea life at the aquarium in Newport."

"I know."

"You do?"

"Yep. Talked to him the other day at the aquarium when I went to see Keiko off. Seems like a nice guy."

Jennie nodded. "He is." Her heart felt like a set of drums. Why were they talking about Scott when all she wanted was for Ryan to apologize and tell her they were still friends?

After another long hesitation he said, "It seems like forever since we've talked."

"Yeah. It does to me too. I've missed it." *I've missed you.* She didn't say the last part out loud.

"Seems like every time we've talked lately I end up having to apologize for something."

"Sounds like you're about to apologize again. Did you do something wrong?" she asked innocently.

"I think we both did."

Jennie started to protest.

"Now, just hear me out. We both got mad at each other. You were upset with me for dating Camilla, and I was really ticked off about Scott."

"I was more hurt than angry," Jennie admitted.

"I think hurt turns into anger and resentment."

"Are you still going out with Camilla?" She probably shouldn't have asked, but she needed to know.

After a long silence he said, "I'm not sure I know how to answer that. Camilla and I have gotten to be good friends. In fact, we're going to a beach party next Saturday night in Lincoln City. A bunch of kids from school are going."

"Ryan, what did you want to talk to me about?" Ryan had been right about one thing. Hurt did turn into anger, and that anger was surfacing right now. "Obviously you didn't call me to kiss and make up."

He chuckled. "Be pretty hard to kiss you over the phone. But if you were here . . ." He left the sentence dangling, then added, "Jennie, I don't want to lose you. We've been friends a long time. I don't want that to change."

"I don't want to lose you either." Jennie closed her eyes and drew in a deep breath.

"Good. I'm not sure I understand what's going on with us. Gram says—"

"Gram? You talked to my grandmother about us?"

"Yeah—she's great. Anyway, I think I have a handle on things now. I'm not jealous of Scott anymore. At least, I'm trying not to be."

"You're not?"

"No. He's a great guy, and I can understand why you'd be attracted to him. You two have a lot in common. You're both passionate about making a difference in the world. I am, too, but I don't even know what I want to do with my life yet. One day I want to fly airplanes, the next I want to teach. I think you've known that you'd go into law enforcement since you were born."

Jennie laughed. "Well, maybe not that long."

"Scott's the same way. He's been an environmentalist since he could talk."

Jennie shrugged. "What's your point?"

"Things are really up in the air for me right now, Jen."

She wished she could see him—talk to him face-to-face. They'd be out on the rocks in front of Gram's place if she were there—gazing out over the ocean. He'd put his arms around her and . . . Jennie eased her mind away from the image as he continued to speak.

"I don't know what I want to be. I don't know who God has in mind for me to marry. Or if I'll even get married." He sighed, and Jennie imagined his gaze linking with hers. "All I'm really sure of right now is that I want us to be friends—or whatever it is we are."

She felt a warmth wash over her. That's exactly what she wanted. "You're right, Ryan. And . . . I'm sorry."

"For what?"

"Acting like a jerk. I feel the same way as you. I really like Scott. We have a lot of fun together when he isn't out saving whales and dolphins and—"

"Jennie?"

"What?"

"I don't want to hear about Scott."

"I thought you were over being jealous."

He laughed. "You know something? Gram was right. She told me that I would probably always feel jealous toward anyone who threatens to come between us."

"I don't think you have to worry about that."

"Really?"

"Yeah. Well, look at us. We're still friends."

"I love you, Jennie McGrady."

"I love you, too, Ryan Johnson."

Jennie smiled from the inside out. She remembered something Gram had told her not all that long ago. *True love will overcome all obstacles.* She wasn't certain if what she and Ryan shared was true love, but they had overcome a major obstacle and at the same time reached a new level in their relationship.

"Hey, Jen?"

"What?"

"Scott told me how you saved his life and managed to find the terrorist who nearly killed him."

"He's exaggerating." Jennie cleared her throat. "You two must have had quite a long conversation."

"Mostly we talked about you. He said he plans to marry you someday."

Jennie about choked. "He did? He said that?"

" 'Fraid so. I told him he'd have to check with me first. That I've known you longer and had first dibs."

She gasped. "You're teasing, right?"

"No way. I'm serious. He said neither one of us would end up marrying you because you'd be too busy solving crimes to plan a wedding."

Jennie rolled her eyes. "He's probably right."

"Are you working on anything exciting right now?"

"Maybe." She told him about Annie and the newspaper caper.

"Sounds like that one's pretty well wrapped up."

"Except for one thing. Annie still seems to think someone has been stalking her. I have a strange feeling she's right." Jennie flopped down on her bed and glanced at the clock. They'd been talking for half an hour. "I should go. I'm expecting a call."

"From Scott?"

"No. From Gavin. He's supposed to be getting a name to go with the license plate on the car that was following Annie."

"Hmm. I'm not sure I like the sound of that. You will be careful, won't you?"

"I always am—well, most of the time."

"Good. I'm thinking it would be great to have you give me my present in person. Either you could come to Bay Village or I'd go to Portland."

"Sounds like a good plan to me."

"So what did you get me?"

"You expect me to tell you?"

"Yeah. What is it? No—don't tell me. A restored Corvette convertible."

"In your dreams, Johnson." She laughed, her heart lighter than it had been in a long time.

After hanging up, Jennie rolled onto her stomach and hugged her pillow. Soon she dozed off and in a half-asleep daze dreamed about Ryan and Scott begging her to marry them. She stepped between them as they nearly came to blows. *"I don't know what to say. I like both of you, but . . ."* She felt a hand on her shoulder. *"My heart belongs to—"*

"Jennie." Dad shook her shoulder. "Hey, princess, wake up. Mom thought you might have to finish up some schoolwork for tomorrow."

"Dad." Jennie stretched and yawned. "You ruined my dream. I was just about to find out who I'm going to marry."

"Marry?!" Dad wrapped his arms around her and kissed her forehead. "I forbid you to ever say that word again." He released her and gave her a teasing smile that pulled at the scar on his handsome face. "At least not until you're thirty. And I get to pick him out."

"Oh, Dad." Jennie hugged him back.

"Princess, I wanted to apologize for not getting back to you on that license plate number you gave me. I gave the information to Rocky. I assume he got back to you on it?"

"He did. Turns out she wasn't following Annie after all." Jennie didn't mention that she didn't share Rocky's opinion.

"I thought that might be the case. You kids need to be careful who you're following. Ms. Noble could easily have filed a complaint against you and Lisa for stalking *her.*"

Jennie's heart stopped. "Noble? Are you saying it was Debra Noble's car?"

Dad frowned. "Rocky didn't tell you?"

"No. He was afraid I might harass her. I wouldn't—"

"Well, I probably shouldn't have said anything. I just assumed . . . Never mind that. Knowing you, you'd have found out anyway. Now that you know, you can forget about it."

"Thanks, Dad." Jennie managed a calm response. Inside, her

mind and stomach were already at work on a myriad of questions.

"Well, I'll leave you to your studies." Her father left, closing the door behind him.

Jennie clasped her hands, barely able to suppress a squeal of delight. She clicked on her bedside lamp and pulled a pad and pen out of the drawer. If the beige Cadillac was registered to Debra Noble, who was driving? Had Debra been wearing a disguise? Had someone borrowed her car? Had Debra been following Annie? If so, why? Maybe Debra was Annie's real mother.

It was crazy. Wild. Bizarre. But what if . . . *No*, Jennie told herself. *It's too soon to be making that kind of assumption.*

Jennie jotted down the questions and made a note to herself to talk to Debra the next day. *You won't be harassing her*, Jennie told herself. *You just want to talk.*

# 12

At seven the next morning Jennie's private telephone rang. She grabbed it on the first ring. It was probably Lisa. Neither she nor Gavin had called the night before, and Jennie's calls to them had only rewarded her with busy signals.

"Hello, Jennie. This is Debra Noble."

"Oh . . . hi." Jennie struggled to keep the shock out of her voice.

"I hope I didn't wake you, but I wanted to catch you before you left for school."

"You didn't." She'd been up for an hour, unable to sleep and wondering how she was going to approach Debra with all her questions. To have the news anchor call out of the blue like this was just plain eerie.

"I tried calling you yesterday—I wanted to thank you for letting me know about Annie. That was a thoughtful thing to do. The interview would have made a good segment, and I thought about running it anyway along with the good news that she'd been located. But the Phillipses thought it would have been too embarrassing for Annie after what she's already been through. I can see their point."

"I thought so too. I'm glad you decided not to run it."

"Yes, well, I certainly hope it all works out for her. She's a sweet girl."

"Yeah." Jennie hesitated. Should she ask her questions now or wait? Later, she decided. She'd ask her face-to-face so she could measure her reaction. But she'd have to be careful. If she let on that she knew Debra owned the car she felt certain had been following Annie, Jennie could get Rocky into trouble. "Um . . . Ms. Noble, I wanted to thank you for televising the stuff about our school and church. It's helped us raise a lot of money."

"Glad to do it. I have been so impressed by the way you people have pulled together, I've decided to join your church."

"Hey, that's great." Was that why Debra's car had been at Trinity yesterday? If so, why the disguise?

"Yes. I was hoping to see you there yesterday to thank you in person."

"I was there. Sorry I missed you. After church we did some family stuff—went to the Harvest Festival."

"Ah. Must be nice to be part of a family."

"Don't you have a family?"

"Not anymore. My parents died in an auto accident last year. I was their only child. I've never married."

"Oh, I'm sorry." She couldn't imagine not having anyone. "Our church is like a family."

"Yes. That's one of the things that drew me. After the fire, everyone pitched in—they have such a strong sense of community." Debra hesitated. "You were instrumental in bringing the arsonist to justice, weren't you, Jennie?"

"Well, sort of. My dad actually made the arrest."

"You're far too modest. I've been doing some more checking on you."

"Me? Why?" Jennie wondered if the checking had anything to do with her and Lisa turning her license number in to the police.

"Curiosity. I'm thinking it might be interesting to interview you for our spotlight on hometown heroes."

Jennie cringed. "I don't think that would be a good idea."

"How about today before your swim practice?"

"I don't think my dad would like it."

"I'll get permission from your parents. We can tie it in with my updates on the school. It'll be a great human interest story."

Jennie didn't want to. She didn't like being in the spotlight. On the other hand, it would get her close to Debra. Maybe before and after the interview she could ask a few questions of her own.

"You're thinking about it. That's good."

Jennie agreed to do the interview as long as her father okayed it. "I don't think there's much chance of that," she added, "but you can ask."

By the time Jennie was ready to leave for school at seven-thirty, Debra had cleared the interview with Jennie's parents and called her back to confirm the time, which would be three-thirty. Jennie would have to hustle to do the interview and make it to swimming on time.

Jennie said good-bye to her mom and Nick, then stepped out onto the porch with her dad. "I can't believe you're letting Debra interview me," Jennie said. "I thought we were supposed to keep a low profile."

Dad had worked as an undercover agent for the DEA to bring down a couple of huge drug cartels in South America. The government assured him that the kingpins who had been out to kill him were in prison. Still, there was always a risk someone would recognize him and retaliate. Of course, revenge was a danger in any law enforcement job.

"I don't think there's much need to worry anymore. And keeping a low profile is next to impossible with you as my daughter. You attract trouble like a magnet. As if that weren't enough, you end up being a champion swimmer."

He walked her out to the car. "Do the interview, princess. Frankly, after what Rocky told me, I'm surprised she's even talking to you. My only real concern here is that she may try to pump you for information about the serial killings. She may think because you're my daughter you'll know more than what we've told the press."

"But I don't know anything—except for what you said in the car yesterday about this last one being a copycat killing."

He settled an arm around her shoulders. "You heard that, did you? See, that's what I mean. It's a hunch on my part, but I don't want anything like that to leak out."

"Don't worry, Dad. If she mentions it, I'll just tell her she needs to talk to you."

"Fair enough."

Jennie waited for her dad to pull out, then backed her Mustang into the street. With every mile she grew more and more excited. Debra Noble had called her, and Jennie planned to take full advantage of the opportunity to find out exactly what the television anchorwoman was doing in a disguise last Friday afternoon and again on Sunday morning.

"Why didn't you call me last night?" Jennie asked the minute Lisa climbed into the car. Jennie usually picked her up on days she had to go in early. Most of the time her mom took her and picked her up.

"I tried—about five times. Have you talked to Gavin yet?" Lisa's eyes blazed with excitement.

"No."

"Well, you're never going to believe who that beige Cadillac is registered to." Lisa had that smug, I-know-something-you-don't look.

"Debra Noble." Jennie grinned at the surprise on Lisa's face.

"How did you—? You lied. You did talk to Gavin."

"No, I swear. Dad told me last night. Not only that, but Debra called me this morning and wants to interview me."

"Why would she want to interview you?"

"She says it's because I caught the arsonist, but Dad thinks she's going to try to get information on the case he's working on."

"Did you ask her if she was following Annie?"

"No. If I talk to her about it, I want to ask her to her face so I can see if she's telling the truth." Jennie braked at the light and tapped the steering wheel to the rhythm of a sixties song on the radio.

"Something isn't right," Lisa said. "I can't believe Debra Noble was following Annie. We must have made a mistake—I mean, why would she?"

"Believe me, I've been asking myself the same question all night."

Lisa's eyes widened. "I just had a crazy idea."

"What?"

"It's too weird, but . . ." Lisa chewed on her bottom lip for several seconds before answering. "What if Debra is Annie's real mom?"

"Interesting." Jennie didn't tell her she'd already had the same notion. "There are definite similarities. They both have dark hair and a small build."

"Their eyes are nearly the exact same shade of blue."

"Debra says she's never been married and doesn't have a family," Jennie mused as she pressed her foot to the gas pedal and eased through the intersection.

"So? That doesn't mean she couldn't have gotten pregnant as a teenager," Lisa persisted.

"I don't know. If she is Annie's mother, then she's the one who threw Annie away. She's a criminal."

"You're right. I don't think Debra Noble is the kind of person who would throw away a baby." Lisa sighed.

"I wish I could just confront her with it and tell her I know she's the one who was following Annie and see what she says. Problem is, if I say anything about it, she'll think Rocky told me."

"Maybe you should just be honest with her—tell her your dad told you."

"Then she'd be upset with Dad. I couldn't do that. She's critical enough of him already."

"Well," Lisa said, "you'll think of something. You always do."

Jennie sighed. "I hope so."

The next seven hours dragged by as Jennie attended two mandatory classes, sat through an especially boring lecture, and completed her homework in the library during fourth period. Since she had the meeting with Debra, it was easier to stay at school than to go home. When the bell rang at three, Jennie raced to the office to pick up her mail, then bolted for the door.

"Jennie! Wait up."

Jennie whirled around and waited for Annie to join her. "I noticed you were back in school today. I wasn't sure you'd come."

"Dad says it's best to face my fears head on. I guess he's right. You were right too. My parents are wonderful people, and I've decided not to let all this stuff about being adopted bother me. I wanted to thank you."

"I didn't do much."

"Yes, you did. You talked me into going home."

"Well, the worst part is over."

"I'm not so sure about that. There's still that business with Charity. She and her mom came over last night to apologize. I feel sorry for her, Jennie. You should have seen her. She's putting on this tough act, but I know inside she's really sad."

"I hope she's learned a lesson. It's hard to imagine anyone being desperate enough to do that."

"She was so embarrassed. She didn't even come to school today."

"I can see why." Jennie glanced toward the door, swarming now with students as anxious as she was to leave. "Look, Annie, I have to go. Debra Noble is doing an interview with me before swimming."

"That's great!"

Jennie nodded and backed toward the door. "I'll see you later."

"Have a good interview."

"Thanks." Jennie didn't tell Annie about the license number belonging to Debra's car. She'd asked Lisa to keep the information secret as well.

An overwhelming sadness settled over her as she thought about Annie. Though she'd said she was doing okay, her eyes told another story. Jennie unlocked the car, opened it, and slid in.

She didn't want to think about Annie right now but offered up a prayer that she would come to accept her circumstances. Jennie directed her mind back to Debra and the interview, asking God to give her the right words to say.

Jennie started the car and made her way through the crowded parking lot to the street. She'd talked to Coach Dayton earlier that day and let her know she might be late. DeeDee didn't sound very happy about it but told Jennie to get there as soon as she could.

Fifteen minutes before her appointment with Debra, Jennie

walked into the lobby of the Channel 22 studios. She announced herself to the receptionist, who made a phone call, probably to Debra, then buzzed her through the security door.

"Ms. Noble's office is just up those stairs—second cubicle on your left."

"Thanks." Jennie took a deep breath for courage and began the ascent. She counted thirty stairs to the landing. There had to be at least that many butterflies fluttering around in her stomach. The vast room was divided into a number of small cubicles. Jennie recognized several faces of people from the Channel 22 News team.

Debra stood beside one of the desks and was talking to a man in a suit and tie. They were laughing about something.

"Excuse me . . ."

"Jennie!" Debra smiled. "Welcome." Turning to the man, she said, "Phil, this is Jennie McGrady. She's the student I'm featuring in our local hero segment today. Jennie, this is Phil Chapman, the co-anchor."

Debra didn't need to introduce him. Jennie had seen him on television so many times, she felt like she knew him. Phil stood and reached for her hand. "Nice to meet you, Jennie. I've heard great things about you."

"Thanks. Nice to meet you too."

"I'll talk to you later, Phil." Turning to Jennie, Debra said, "I'm glad you're early. I'd like to see you privately before we actually do the interview." She glanced around. "There's no one in the conference room. It'll be quiet in there."

Debra sat in one of ten chairs around a large oval table and indicated for Jennie to sit next to her. Was it Jennie's imagination, or did Debra seem nervous? The reporter clenched her hands, brought them to her chin as if saying a prayer, then lowered them to her lap.

"I . . . I'd like to clear something up before we do the interview. First, let me say that I did not choose to interview you because you are Detective McGrady's daughter. I don't intend to pump you for information about the murders."

Jennie frowned. "I wouldn't have any to give you." She found it odd that Debra would mention it; then the light dawned. "My dad called you, didn't he?"

Debra gave a half nod. "Yes, he did. He told me in no uncertain terms that he didn't want me using you to get to him. I assured him that wasn't my intention." She tilted her head. "He told me something else as well. He said I should talk to you about . . . well, about an incident that nearly got me into trouble with the police."

"Incident . . . oh, you mean my turning over your license number to them?" Jennie fiddled with the strap on her backpack.

"Yes. Officer Rockwell suggested the same thing. Both of them indicated you were a determined young lady and that I might be better off telling you the truth rather than trying to keep you at bay. I'm afraid you caught me in a rather embarrassing situation."

# 13

"I don't understand." Jennie brought her gaze up to meet Debra's.

Debra smiled, then shifted her gaze from Jennie to the table, then back again, not quite making eye contact. "The person you saw driving that beige Cadillac last Friday was me, but I wasn't following Annie. I was heading for the mall and just happened to be behind Annie and her boyfriend."

"Why the wig and sunglasses?"

"For protection. I'm sure you can understand my predicament. I'm fairly well known, and when I go out, invariably people want my autograph or to talk to me about something. It usually entails their ideas on how I can do my job better. So when I go out in public to run personal errands, I'll often wear a wig and sunglasses. Friday was one of those days. I'm not sure why you thought I was following Annie. I'd have no reason to do that. In fact, I've had the experience of being stalked myself. I wouldn't wish that on anyone."

"You came out of a side street near the school and turned in behind her." Jennie eyed her suspiciously. "Are you saying I jumped to conclusions?"

She licked her lips. "I'm afraid you did."

"What about yesterday—at church. You were wearing your disguise then too?"

"Yes. As I said, I don't like appearing in public."

"So you weren't at church because you thought Annie might be there."

"No—of course not."

Debra was lying. Jennie could see it in her eyes. But why would she? Unless . . . "You have two cars," Jennie said. "The teal van and the Cadillac."

"Yes. I inherited the Caddy from my parents when they died. I've never had the heart to get rid of it. I keep it in the garage and take it out when I'm in disguise."

"I thought you said they died in an auto accident."

"They did. The Cadillac was their second car."

"I still think you were following Annie, and I think I know why. Lisa and I were talking this morning about how much you and Annie look alike."

"We do?" The statement caught her off guard.

"Sure—you even have some of the same mannerisms. We wondered if you might be her real mom."

Debra closed her eyes. She looked ready to cry. "Oh, Jennie, I wish more than anything that were the case." She drew in a deep breath. "Your father was right. You are persistent."

"Only when I know I'm right."

"I see." Debra pushed her chair back, got up, and walked to the window. She folded her arms and tipped her head back.

Jennie wasn't sure what to say or do. She'd clearly over-stepped her boundaries and wondered if Rocky would consider her comments as harassment. "I guess you won't want to inter-view me now. Maybe I should go."

"No. Stay." Debra turned back around. "You were right about one thing, Jennie. I was following Annie that day—not fol-lowing her, exactly, just . . . I can't explain it. I feel drawn to her. You are right. She does look like me—she looks like she could be my daughter."

Jennie sat quietly, waiting for her to go on. Gram had taught her that when you keep quiet, people will often give you more information than they might otherwise. Silence makes them nervous and they talk. All you have to do is listen.

"Only she isn't. You're completely wrong about that," Debra went on. "For one thing, I could never do what Annie's birth mother did. Of course, some people would think what I did was ten times worse. At least Annie lived. My baby didn't."

"You said you'd never married."

"I hadn't. My boyfriend left me when I told him I was pregnant. I was only seventeen at the time. My parents were on one of their long trips to Europe. I didn't have the heart to tell them. I had every intention of giving birth and giving the baby up for adoption. But as the time came closer, I panicked. What would I tell my parents? I went to a doctor, and he told me it wasn't too late to have an abortion. I . . . I agreed."

Jennie didn't know what to say. How terrible it must have been to be faced with a decision like that.

"You're pro-life, aren't you?" Debra paced back and forth in front of the window.

"Yes."

"So am I—now. Back then I didn't think much about it one way or the other. Abortion was legal, so it must be okay. I wanted to go to college and have a career. My parents would never have forgiven me. Besides, they were older and basically unavailable. Being alone and unmarried, I felt it was the best option at the time. The doctor was so kind. He even—" She shook her head. "I never thought the aftereffects of having an abortion would be so painful. He told me it would be a simple procedure—I'd have some labor pains, but the fetus was still small and I wouldn't suffer too much. He neglected to mention that aborting my baby would leave a hole in my heart the size of China. I took the easy way out, or so I thought. I told myself it was for the best, and the doctor agreed."

She stopped and pressed both hands on the table in front of Jennie. "Even with all that, I made the wrong choice. Not a day goes by that I don't regret my decision. I look at every child with longing in my heart. The doctor didn't tell me if it was a boy or a girl. I never asked. So you see, Jennie, Annie's birth mother may have put her into the trash, but she did call the police, and Annie was rescued. I murdered mine." Tears filled her blue eyes.

"I'm sorry." Jennie wanted to tell her it wasn't her fault, that it wasn't really murder . . . but would she be right? Somehow she didn't think so—not when she thought of the tiny baby growing inside her own mother's uterus.

"So am I, Jennie. You will never know how sorry I am."

Debra straightened and went back to the window.

"Why did you follow Annie?" Jennie asked. "If you had an abortion . . ."

"I'm not sure. When I first saw her, my heart felt as though it would explode. I know intellectually that Annie isn't remotely related to me and that she couldn't possibly be my child. Wishful thinking, I suppose. I'd like to think the abortion didn't happen and that my baby is still alive. All I know is that when I saw Annie's picture in the paper after she and the others were elected to the Fall Festival Court, my heart melted. I wanted to know more about her. I obtained her records and found out she'd been discarded by her mother, then adopted by the Phillipses. I know she isn't mine, but I can still dream."

Debra glanced at her watch and came back to the table. "We need to go. I hope I can trust you not to mention our discussion to anyone. I'm not sure why I even told you all that. You're a good listener."

"I'm glad you did. And don't worry. Your secret is safe with me." *As long as you leave Annie alone,* she added to herself. Jennie had an odd feeling in the pit of her stomach. She believed Debra now, but there was more to it than that. If she could trust her intuition—and she often could—this case was far from being solved.

Jennie picked up her bag and followed Debra out the door and down the hall. Four agonizing minutes later they began the interview. Jennie wished she hadn't come. She wished she had Lisa's taste in clothes and her petite figure. She wished she had Allison's poise. She wished she could stop worrying about making a fool of herself and that her mouth wouldn't feel so dry. Jennie wiped her sweaty palms on her jeans. *Jeans—good grief.* She should have had Lisa pick something out for her. She hadn't even thought about her clothes—she just grabbed something clean. Her shirt was okay, a white knit with a V neck. *Calm down, McGrady.* She tried giving herself a pep talk. *You look fine. You're here now, and you are not going to back down, so make the most of it. There are only a few hundred thousand people watching. People who might help to restore Trinity's losses.*

"Relax, Jennie," Debra interrupted her thoughts. "You'll do

fine. You're an inspiration, and I know there are kids out there—adults too—who will admire your courage."

*Courage?* Jennie felt anything but courageous. She'd have preferred stepping into a snake pit. As long as they weren't poisonous. She shivered at the thought and looked at the cameras trained on her and Debra. Well, maybe not snakes.

Debra began by introducing Jennie as a student at Trinity High and reminded the audience about the arson fire. "Over the past few weeks we've seen the church community rebuild and flourish. I think that's largely due to the quality of the people involved. They don't back down in the face of tragedy. If anything, they come back stronger than ever. They are survivors. Jennie McGrady is one of those survivors. She is, in my opinion, a hero. Jennie has achieved excellence in sports as well as academics."

Jennie wasn't sure she liked where the conversation was going. With every accolade she felt herself growing smaller and her cheeks growing more red.

"Jennie, I understand you plan to go into law enforcement."

"That's right. I'd like to get a law degree."

"So you plan to become a lawyer?"

"I'm not sure. My mother would prefer that to my being a cop. I'd like to do something more . . ."

"Adventurous?"

"Yeah."

Debra then went on to ask several more questions about her family. As they talked, Jennie began to relax. Though she did mention that Detective Jason McGrady was Jennie's father and was working on the triple-murder investigation, she didn't ask Jennie about the investigation itself.

Toward the end of the interview, Debra brought up Jennie's success on the swim team. "Your coach tells me you could compete in the Olympics if you chose to. Any plans on going for the gold?"

"It takes a lot of commitment to be an Olympic athlete. I'm not sure I'd want to do that. My mom's having a baby soon and needs my help. I enjoy swimming, but I'm not sure I want to put that much effort into sports—at least not now."

Debra asked a few more questions about the meet, then went on to Jennie's involvement in several criminal investigations.

Jennie felt uncomfortable talking about her investigative skills, and when Debra asked about them, Jennie shrugged and said, "I'm just curious, I guess. I don't like to see people getting away with things. I suppose that's why I want to go into law enforcement. I think criminals should be caught and punished. There are too many people today literally getting away with murder."

"I'd like to explore that further with you, but our time is up. You are an amazing young woman, Jennie. Thanks for taking time out of your busy schedule to talk with us."

"No problem." Jennie smiled into the camera until the producer signaled an end to the session.

Debra thanked her again off the air. "Before you go, I wonder if you have any thoughts about the pro-life murders?"

Jennie tensed. "I don't know much about them. Anyway, I thought you weren't going to ask me about that."

"Not on the air. And I'm not grilling you, am I?" Without waiting for an answer, she said, "In each case the victim was a known and vocal pro-life advocate. The killer always leaves a calling card—did you know that? You didn't, did you? Most people don't."

When Jennie didn't answer, she said, "It's frightening what some people do for a political cause. Do you suppose the murders are retaliation against the protest marches and bombings of abortion clinics?"

"I really don't know." Jennie swallowed hard. "What are you getting at?"

"To be honest, Jennie, I'm not sure. I don't know if you are aware of this, but I have made my pro-life stand public on a number of occasions. I volunteer at one of the crisis pregnancy centers run by our local Right to Life organization."

"So you think you're in danger—that you could be next?"

"There is that possibility."

"Maybe you should ask the police for protection."

Debra tossed her an incredulous look. "Don't get me wrong, Jennie. I respect our men in blue. But I know exactly what they'd say—there's no way we can offer protection to all the possible victims. There's no reason why it should be me and not some of the others, except that I've gotten pretty vocal lately."

"I don't know what to say. I hope you've got a good security system, and maybe you should hire a bodyguard."

"I've thought of that. And I'm having a security system installed tomorrow."

Jennie excused herself, and Debra told her she'd like to talk to her later.

During her trip to swim practice, Jennie worried over what to tell Lisa and Gavin. She shouldn't have gotten them involved in checking out the license number. She didn't want to lie to them, but she couldn't betray Debra's confidence either.

Once in the pool, Jennie tried to set her concerns aside and empty her mind of everything but swimming laps. The water worked its usual miracle, easing away the tension and clearing her head. The one thing she couldn't seem to shake was the gut feeling that something terrible was about to happen. The problem with intuition, or a sixth sense, as Gram often called it, was that you didn't know what would happen or whom it would happen to. *"All you can do is pray,"* Gram had told her. *"And let God take care of the rest."*

During the next two laps Jennie did pray. *I don't know what's going on, God, but if I'm right, someone is going to get hurt. Protect whoever it is.*

When she came up, a whistle shrilled and echoed through the pool area. "Come on, Jennie," DeeDee yelled. "You can do better. Take a break and next time put some effort into it."

"Sorry," Jennie mumbled. She hauled herself up and swung around to sit on the ledge. Her arms felt like mush.

"Hey, Jennie." Russ sat down beside her. "Don't feel bad— we all have our off days."

She grinned. "I guess this is one of mine." She glanced at the stands, where Annie and Lisa were sitting with several other students and parents. "Looks like Annie's gotten over her crisis."

"Shawn says she's faking it. I think she's trying, but this adoption thing is tearing her apart inside."

"You can't blame her for being upset. It'll take time, but she'll come around."

"Yeah—maybe. I just hope it isn't too late. Shawn is losing his patience." He slipped into the water and swam away.

Jennie got out, dried off, and headed for the stands. Something about Russ's remark made her wonder if Annie and Shawn had been arguing.

"I don't care what the coach says. You look great out there." Lisa curled a strand of her hair around her finger.

"Thanks, but she's right. I wasn't concentrating—at least, not on swimming."

"How did your interview with Debra go?" Annie asked.

Jennie shrugged. "Good—I guess. I'm not much for that sort of thing."

"I can't wait to see it." Annie's smile faded. "Jennie . . . um . . . I've been thinking. I'd really like to find my birth mom, and I want you to help me."

# 14

Jennie winced. "I'm not sure trying to find your birth mother is a good idea, Annie."

"Maybe not, but I need to know what happened and why she couldn't keep me. Mom and Dad said she was probably young and couldn't take care of me. I need to know what she's like—I want to know who I am and where I came from. Shawn thinks I'm crazy, but I feel like it's something I have to do."

"You're not crazy—it's just not a good plan. I really doubt she will want to be found. She's still wanted by the police."

"I know, but I have to try. I'm not who I thought I was. Please, Jennie, will you help me?"

"Have you told your parents? Seems like they're in a better position to find out than I am. After all, your dad was there when they brought you into the hospital."

"No—and don't you tell them. It would just upset them."

"I don't know. I'll have to think about it."

"They gave me an album. It has newspaper articles in it and Mom's journal about me. I don't know if it will be much help."

Jennie drew in a deep breath. "I guess it wouldn't hurt to look at it. If the police had any clues, though, I'm sure they would have found her."

"Jennie," DeeDee called from across the pool. "You're up for the 500—see if you can better your record."

"Coming." Turning back to Lisa and Annie she said, "We'll talk later."

---

At six-thirty, Jennie dragged herself from the car to the house. She'd managed a decent performance at swim practice but couldn't seem to clock as good a time as she had before. Her mind weighed heavily with Annie and her request. After practice she'd taken Lisa home and promised to call Annie later. She didn't have a good feeling about it. But then, what else was new?

Mom set a bowl of salad on the kitchen table as Jennie came in. There was only one setting at the table.

"Where's Dad?"

"He came home for an early dinner, then went back to work." A fleeting look of worry crossed her face.

"Did he say why?" Jennie climbed onto the stool at the bar.

She shook her head. "No, but I'm sure it has something to do with the murder investigation he's been working so hard on. He's getting a lot of pressure to find this serial killer before he strikes again."

Jennie gave her a hug and inhaled the spicy aroma of whatever Mom had been cooking. "Smells good. What is it?"

"You're favorite—spaghetti with meat sauce."

"Mommy," Nick called from upstairs. "I'm done with my bath."

Mom pulled a plate out of the cupboard. "Would you be a dear and get Nick out of the tub and into his pajamas? I'll dish up the rest of your dinner."

"Sure." Jennie sauntered out of the kitchen, through the dining room and entry, then took the stairs two at a time. It felt good to see Mom happy and healthy again. Well, mostly happy. She was worried about Dad—Jennie was too.

"Hey, buddy, are you sure you had water in that tub? All I can see are toys."

He rolled his eyes. "I letted the water out. Can't you see I'm all wet? I even washeded my hair."

"Yeah, but you forgot to rinse it."

"No, I didn't."

She took his hand and put it on his head. "Feel that gooey stuff? It's shampoo."

"Oh." He gave her a sheepish grin.

"Hey, don't feel bad. You got most of it out. When hair is as thick as ours, you gotta rinse it a bunch of times."

"You gonna pour water over my head?"

"Yep. Close your eyes." Jennie rinsed his hair while he sputtered, then helped him out of the tub. Wrapping him in a towel, she gave him a hug and a smoochy kiss. "You smell like bubbles."

"That's 'cause I put bubbles in there."

"You are too cute." She towel-dried his hair and wrapped him in the towel again, then carried him into his room. "Come on, let's get you dressed."

"I can dress myself," he said importantly when she set him down. "You go away now so I can have some piracy."

Jennie chuckled. "You mean privacy."

"That's what I said. Now go!" He was getting to the age where he didn't want help with much of anything.

"Okay, I'm going." While Jennie understood his need to become more independent, she missed taking care of him. She was going to enjoy having a new baby around.

Jennie went back downstairs, attacked her dinner, then, after helping Nick with a puzzle, headed upstairs to do her homework. When she finished that, she would call Annie.

Five minutes into her reading assignment for history, her eyes drifted closed. She'd made the mistake of sitting on her bed with her head resting against her pillow. Jennie let the book slide off her lap and onto the floor. She scooted down, fluffed up her pillow, and gave into the exhaustion she'd been feeling all day.

When she woke up it was dark, the room filled with shadows. Without turning on the light, Jennie got out of bed and went to sit in the window seat. The half-moon illuminated the gold and red leaves lingering on the big oak tree. She leaned her head against the window, thinking of her conversation with Debra earlier, then with Annie. She wondered if it was still early enough to call, but she made no move to do so. Instead, she watched a leaf flutter and drift to the ground.

Drifting. That's how Jennie felt at the moment. Disconnected. She closed her eyes. A wariness still lingered in her mind—that sixth sense of hers predicting danger without giving any details.

"Princess? You in here?"

Jennie's heart jumped to her throat.

"Dad! You scared me." Jennie willed her heart back in her chest. "I didn't hear you come in. What are you doing—what time is it?"

"Almost eleven. Your mom said you'd fallen asleep doing your homework. She asked if I'd check on you."

"Oh. I'm okay." She stretched and yawned. "Just sleepy."

"You looked deep in thought. Anything you want to talk about?"

"Uh . . . no. Not really." Jennie wished she could tell him about the conversation she'd had with Debra, but she wouldn't—not yet.

"Well, if you change your mind, I'll be downstairs. I'm going to watch the news before I turn in."

When her dad left, she turned on the light, then sat on her bed and waited for her eyes to adjust. She undid her braid and picked her book off the floor. She'd have to set her alarm early and do her math assignment in the morning. It would be just like Mrs. Wish to give them a pop quiz.

More awake now, Jennie went downstairs to the kitchen and poured herself a glass of juice.

Her father had stretched out in his recliner. With the remote he turned on the television set, then muted a car commercial. He shifted his weary gaze to Jennie.

"Looks like you had a rough day," Jennie said.

"I've had better. Yours was good, though, I hear. I saw the interview you did with Ms. Noble. Nice job. Your mom recorded it. Want to watch it?"

Jennie wrinkled her nose. "I lived through it once—that's enough."

"I imagine it is. You're like me in that regard." The news came on, and Dad clicked the mute off.

Phil, the news anchor she'd met at the station, opened the segment. "Police are continuing their investigation into the murders of the three pro-life leaders. So far they have no suspects in the case. Channel 22 has just had word that the killer may have attempted to strike again."

Jennie's dad snapped his recliner up. "What?"

"Our own Debra Noble is the killer's most recent target."

# 15

Jennie froze. "This can't be happening."

"Fortunately," the news anchor went on to say, "Debra was able to escape. She's on the scene now."

"I don't believe this." Dad was on his feet and reaching for his cell phone.

Jennie couldn't believe it either. Only that afternoon Debra had expressed fear that she might be next. Now this. Without taking her eyes off the screen, Jennie sank onto the couch.

The camera shifted to a close-up of Debra Noble standing in front of a squad car with its lights flashing. Behind them was a house with the door open and several police officers milling around. The crime scene had already been secured with yellow tape.

"Tell us what happened out there, Debra," Phil said.

"It's been a harrowing evening, Phil. I came home at nine-thirty, and my house had been ransacked. At first I thought I'd been robbed, but then I realized someone was still in the house. I ran to the neighbors and called the police, but by the time they arrived, the intruder was gone."

"How do you know it was the serial killer?"

She placed a hand on her heart. "The police found the same kind of sick note on my desk that the serial killer left pinned to his victims. He was apparently planning to kill me."

"What's going on?" Detective McGrady barked into the phone. "Why wasn't I notified?"

"Did you get a look at him, Debra?" Phil asked.

"No, Phil, unfortunately not. All I could think of was to get as far away as possible and call the police. It's been a terrifying experience, but the police are hopeful that the killer got careless this time and left some leads. I can tell you one thing—after tonight, I'm hiring a bodyguard."

Phil thanked her and moved on to report another bank robbery in downtown Portland.

Jennie rubbed her arms. Was this why she'd had that uneasy feeling all day? Maybe she should have taken Debra's comments more seriously.

"So when were you planning to let me know?" Dad grabbed his suit jacket off the chair and shrugged into it. "Yeah. I'm on my way."

"Dad?"

"Not now, honey. I have to get over to Ms. Noble's house."

"I want to come."

"I don't think—"

"Today after the interview, Debra told me she thought she'd be next. Please let me come with you. You need to hear this."

He hesitated, then nodded. "All right. I'll write your mom a note in case she wakes up and finds us gone. But hurry."

Jennie raced upstairs, grabbed her shoes and a sweat shirt, and made a beeline for the car.

"Tell me what she said." Dad wasted no time in getting to the point.

After pulling on her sweat shirt and settling back against the seat, Jennie repeated the conversation she'd had with Debra after the taping. "Do you think maybe she was having a premonition or something?"

"Or something," he muttered.

Jennie frowned. "You don't think she's making this up, do you?"

"Think about it, Jennie. She talks to you about the possibility, telling you she fits the profile of the other victims. She wants police protection, so she fakes an attack to get it. You heard her—she didn't see the intruder—apparently no one did."

"I don't think she'd do that."

"Gut feeling?"

"Yeah." She met his challenge head on. "A gut feeling."

"Okay. You know her better than I do. Let's see what you think after we talk to her."

Jennie suppressed a smile, pleased that he would take her seriously.

Her father pulled up behind several other squad cars and jumped out. Jennie tagged along behind her dad as he wove through the crowd. Debra was sitting in one of the squad cars in the driveway, drinking a cup of coffee. Jennie's father got a report from one of the officers that pretty much matched Debra's story. Lab people were going over the house looking for clues.

When she saw Jennie and Detective McGrady, Debra left the car and walked toward them. She was still wearing the pink suit and matching heels she'd been wearing during their interview. "Well, if it isn't the detective and his famous daughter. Wasn't I right, Jennie?" She sighed. Turning to Jennie's dad she said, "I suppose you want me to tell you what happened too."

"Is there anything I should know that you didn't tell your viewing audience?"

"Not really. I didn't see anyone." She ran a shaky hand through her already messy hair. "I came in as usual, saw the mess, and—" She bit her lip and closed her eyes for a moment as if to regain her composure. "I was about to go inside when I heard a noise."

"You live alone?"

"Yes."

"Any pets?"

"Do you mean did my cat make the noise I heard? No. I wish that were the case. Puddie was sitting beside the door meowing when I opened it. I picked her up. That's when I heard it."

"Can you describe the sound?"

"I know exactly what it was. He was opening the closet door in my bedroom. It squeaks." She shuddered and took another sip of the coffee.

"I'm going to have a look around," Dad said. "Jennie, do you want to come with me or stay out here with Debra?"

"I . . . um . . ." She apologized to Debra. "It's not often I get to see a crime scene, Ms. Noble. If you don't mind . . ."

"Go ahead. Maybe you can find something the police can't." She ducked back into the police car and stared straight ahead, sipping at the coffee and looking as though she wanted to cry but trying to stay together for the camera.

Two officers were inside gathering evidence. Dad talked briefly to one, then turned to Jennie. "We can walk through," he said. "Just make sure you don't touch anything."

They walked across the wood floor of the entry and took a left into an office. Files from the two metal cabinets were strewn all over the floor, the drawers of her desk flung out and emptied. On top of the desk was the note Debra had mentioned. It had been typed in bold print on plain white paper. All it said was *Pro-choice rules!*

As they continued through the house, Jennie felt a sense of déjà vu and an overwhelming sympathy for Debra. Her own room had been ripped apart like this only a couple of months before. She'd felt violated, angry, and terrified. Debra must have been feeling much the same.

The intruder had pulled out every drawer and emptied its contents on the floor. They emerged from the bedroom and picked their way over to the living room. The white leather cushions had been thrown off the sofa and chair. Throw pillows in shades of peach and green were scattered about the room. Several plants lay on the taupe carpet, dirt scattered, leaves and vines trampled. In the corner, near an upended magazine rack, Jennie noticed a partial footprint in the dirt. A man's print.

"Careful." Her father drew her back, then knelt down for a closer look. "You may be right, princess. I don't think our Ms. Noble did this. But I don't believe our serial killer did either."

"Why?"

"This is a dress shoe. Probably a smooth leather finish on the bottom. It doesn't match the print we found outside the first victim's house."

"What about the note?"

"Hard to say. Each time the killer used a different brand of paper and typeface. Words are similar."

"Could he have changed shoes too?"

"Yep. We'll check out the shoe size. Which means exactly nothing. The guy could be wearing different sizes to throw us off the track. Or it could be a woman wearing men's shoes."

"Or a woman with big feet."

"Exactly."

Going back outside, Dad stopped to talk with Debra again.

"Do you have anyone you can stay with tonight? Friends, family?"

She shook her head. "I have no family. My closest friend, Jillian, is away. I don't know anyone else well enough, but I don't need to stay anywhere. I need to stay here and straighten this mess up."

"You won't be able to get back in there for another day or so. For your safety and your emotional well-being, it would be best if you stayed clear of the place for a while."

She swallowed. "Yes, of course. You're right. I . . . I suppose I could check into a motel."

"Dad." Jennie nudged him and took him aside. "I don't think she should be alone. Why don't we let her stay with us? She can use the spare room."

He glanced at Debra. For a moment Jennie didn't think he'd agree. "That might not be a bad idea, princess. She looks pretty shaken. In fact"—he handed Jennie his car keys—"you could take her there now. I'll get a ride with Smith."

Smith was one of the officers standing outside. Jennie took the keys and went back to Debra.

Dad followed. "Ms. Noble, you're welcome to stay with us."

"Oh, that's very nice, but I couldn't."

"Yes, you can," Jennie interjected. "We have a guest room, and you'd be safe there. Anyway, didn't you say you wanted to be a member of Trinity?"

"Well, yes, but what does that have to do with—"

"We're part of the Trinity family, which means you're part of our family too."

"But your mother—she'd be upset."

Jennie smiled. "My mom would be upset if you *didn't* come. Trust me on this."

"She's right," Dad said.

Debra swung her legs out of the car. "All right. Um . . . Detective McGrady, do you suppose I could get some clothes?"

"Sure. The guys are finished in the bedroom. I'll go in with you."

Jennie paced back and forth while she waited, partly out of nerves and partly to keep warm. Fall was definitely here with temperatures dropping into the mid-forties. The chill permeated her sweat shirt.

Her dad's cell phone rang as he and Debra came back outside. Debra had changed and was now wearing jeans and a sweater. She slipped on a burgundy jacket. Dad escorted her down the steps and stopped next to Jennie. With his cell phone pressed against his ear, he held up a hand to them, signaling them to stay put and to be quiet. His frown deepened as he listened. "Is that right? How can I be sure you're telling me the truth?"

He ran a hand down his face and looked at his watch. "Okay. I can probably do that. Hang on a minute, let me get a pen. I want to be sure I get the information right."

Dad pulled a pen and note pad out of his pocket and began writing. "Uh-huh. Right." He looked over at Debra. "Yeah, now let me read that back to you to make sure I got it all down the way you want it. You want me to tell Debra Noble that it wasn't you who broke into her house. And you want her to go on television and retract her statements. If she doesn't, you *will* kill her."

# 16

Jennie stood wide-eyed with her mouth hanging open, trying to figure out what was going on. Then it hit her. The caller must be the serial killer. Dad was trying to keep him on the line so his call could be traced.

"Okay," Dad went on as though he were having a normal conversation. "Yeah, I don't blame you for being upset. You say you weren't responsible for the last murder, and you don't want to be accused of killing more people than you've actually killed. Can't fault you for that. You have standards, right?"

After another hesitation, Dad nodded. "Yes, sir. I will do that. Listen, while I have you on the phone, I think it might be a good idea for you to give yourself up. You know we're going to catch you sooner or later. It'll be easier for you now."

Dad tucked the pen and pad into his pocket. "I see. I guess I can understand that. Don't want to quit until the job is done. How many more do you have to go?"

He tipped his head back and rubbed his neck. "That many. Well, now, I don't think we can let you do that. You may not agree with their philosophy, but killing them isn't going to . . ."

Dad clicked off the phone and folded it. He blew out a long breath. "That, in case you hadn't guessed, was our serial killer. Seems he has a bone to pick with you, Ms. Noble."

"Did you keep him on the line long enough to trace the call?" Jennie asked.

"Hopefully."

The cell phone rang again. Dad's grin stretched wide across

his face. "Good job." He took out his pen and wrote a note on his palm. "Get someone out to his house right away. Tell them to stay put until I get there. No sirens. I don't want to spook the guy."

"Jennie, take Ms. Noble to the house."

"No way, McGrady." Debra faced him, hands on her hips. "I'm coming with you. I want this story."

"You'll get it. Like I said, I don't want to chance losing him. I'll let you know as soon as we have him in custody." He spun around and nabbed one of the officers. A split second later they were tearing down the street.

"Let's follow them." Debra grabbed Jennie's keys out of her hand and raced to the car. Before Jennie could stop her, Debra had the car running. Leaning out the window, she said, "Are you coming?"

Jennie hit her fist against the fender as she raced around to the passenger side. She got in and slammed the door. Debra accelerated.

"This is stupid. You don't even know where he's going. And you can't possibly catch him."

Debra tossed Jennie a wicked grin. "Oh, but I do. I saw your dad write down the address." She laughed. "Come on, Jennie, you're as eager to be there when they make the arrest as I am."

"Maybe so, but my dad is going to hit the roof."

"I'll take full responsibility." She slowed for a light near the freeway entrance. "Besides, I think he'll be expecting us."

"Humph." Jennie folded her arms and slammed back against the seat, outwardly annoyed but secretly pleased to be in on the action.

"Do you have a cell phone in here?"

"Yeah. This is my mom's car. Dad insists she have one for emergencies."

"Good. Dial the station for me. I need the camera crew to meet me." She rattled off the number. Jennie dialed and handed Debra the phone.

They entered the I-205 freeway and headed south. When Debra handed the phone back, Jennie asked, "Where are we going?"

"Just west of Tualatin."

By the time they arrived, there were at least a dozen cars from the local police department, the sheriff's office, and the state patrol. The Channel 22 News van pulled in behind Debra and Jennie. A young man in his twenties, with spiked blond hair and dark roots, was being dragged from the house by two uniformed officers.

Dad came out behind them. He glanced at Jennie and Debra but didn't look surprised to see them. He didn't seem angry either.

The young man glared at Debra, then spat toward them and swore. "I'll get you, you witch. If it hadn't been for you—"

"All right, that's enough." Dad stepped between the man and Jennie as if to shield her from his barbs. "Get him out of here."

One of the officers helped him into the backseat of a squad car.

While Debra interviewed Detective McGrady and the rest of the crew got footage of the scene, Jennie leaned against the car. Murderers, she decided, came in all sorts of packages. She rubbed her arms to ward off the chill that emanated from the suspect's ice-blue eyes.

From the backseat of the patrol car, the man looked up to catch her watching him and looked away. The vehemence was gone now, a smug smile in its place.

That made Jennie shiver even more. Had his threat been meant for her as well as Debra? As long as he was in jail, she needn't worry. But what if he escaped? Or what if the police didn't have enough evidence to convict him?

After the interview with Jennie's dad, Debra came back to Jennie and handed her the keys. "Time to go home, Jennie." Dad had gone with Smith to take their prisoner in. "Your dad says it's going to be a long night and you need to get some sleep."

---

"Jennie," Mom's voice drifted into her brain. "Come on, sweetheart—it's ten already."

"Ten?" She sat up. "My alarm—I'm late."

Mom laughed. "You're fine. All you're missing is an assembly. I called Mrs. Talbot to say you wouldn't be in, and she said your chemistry lab was canceled anyway."

Jennie sank back onto the pillows. "Oh. Thanks for letting me sleep in."

"You're welcome." Mom sat on the bed, and Jennie scooted her leg out of the way. "Just don't let it happen again."

"But, Mom, it wasn't my fault. Dad—"

"I know." Mom sighed. "Your father shouldn't have taken you with him."

"So is Dad in trouble?"

Mom reached over and brushed a strand of hair from Jennie's forehead. "Big time. No dessert for a week." Mom's cheeks dimpled.

"That should do it." Jennie yawned. "Is Debra still here?"

"Yes. Poor thing, she's exhausted. Fortunately, she doesn't have to be in to work today until two. Give her a chance to recuperate. I'm glad you suggested she stay here."

"Me too." Jennie rubbed the sleep from her eyes. "Guess I'd better get up."

Mom scooted off the bed. "Oh." She grabbed her stomach.

"What's wrong?"

Mom laughed. "Nothing. You're worse than your father. The baby just kicked me."

"Really?"

"Mmm. Third time this morning. I think he's doing his morning exercises."

"That's so cool."

Jennie was still smiling when she kissed her mother good-bye and headed for school. Funny how something so small as a baby's kick could make your day.

At school Jennie heard bits and pieces about the special assembly, but she didn't get the entire story until lunch.

"So where were you?" Lisa asked.

"It's a long story. I'll tell you later."

"You should have been here, Jen." B.J. Beaumont took a bite out of her taco and started to talk around it.

"B.J., mind your manners." Allison gave her sister a playful punch. "What she's trying to say is that Charity gave a public apology to Annie and everyone at the school—especially Gavin and the journalism department. She's dropped out of the running for Fall Festival Queen and said she hopes Annie wins."

"Only I don't think she will," Lisa said. "She's been acting so weird. She and Shawn had a huge argument today."

"Why?"

"Well, you know she wants us to help her find her mom. Shawn thinks it's stupid."

"That's not why they were fighting." Allison's perfect blond hair swung as she glanced around. "The real reason is that after the assembly Shawn was talking to Charity."

"Well, that too." Lisa took a sip of milk. "Charity and Shawn used to date. I think he was just telling her he was proud of her for talking to the group like that."

"It did take a lot of courage," Allison agreed. "Still, I don't think Shawn should have hugged her. That was his mistake."

"He hugged her?" Jennie unwrapped her taco and spread on a dab of hot sauce.

"Annie came unglued," B.J. said. "Told Shawn she never wanted to see him again and walked out."

Jennie held the taco midair. "She left the school?"

"Yep."

"Where is she now?"

Lisa shrugged. "No one knows. The school has called her parents."

Jennie groaned. "Don't tell me she's run away again."

"I hope not," Lisa said. "I thought she was going to be okay with this. She was even seeing a counselor."

"How can she be?" B.J. said. Tossing her napkin down, she got up from the table and stomped off.

Allison looked after her. "She's really feeling upset right now. I think it's all those years of not knowing her real dad even existed. She knows what it's like to feel lost."

"What about you, Allison?" Jennie asked. "You never knew your mother."

"That's true, but I did have my real dad, and I knew from the beginning that my stepmom had adopted me. And even if I wanted to see my mom, I couldn't. She's dead." Allison pinched her lips together. "I have her pictures, though. Dad told me about her—the way she was before she left him. I'm just glad my mother didn't take me with her. B.J. definitely got the worse end of the deal."

"So am I." Lisa wiped her hand with a napkin. "I just hope Annie can get through this. Maybe if you and B.J. talked to her."

"It's worth a try, isn't it?" Allison dipped a fork into her salad. "I'll call her tonight."

Jennie felt terrible. She hadn't called Annie back the night before and hadn't been at the assembly this morning. She wished she could help find Annie's mom, but that would take a miracle.

Jennie finished her lunch and managed to make it through her afternoon class, then went to the library, where she pulled out the materials Annie had given her after the meet the day before and began to read through the various articles. She tried to get a picture of the area in which Annie was found. The Dumpster where she'd been placed was only a few miles from school. Maybe she could go there and see it. In sixteen years things would have changed. Jennie doubted the trash bin would even be there. Still, it was worth a try.

Jennie checked her mailbox and left. Out in the car, she opened her backpack and pulled out the clipping she'd gotten from Annie. She had no trouble finding the store—an older mom-and-pop kind of place that definitely needed fixing up. A trash bin sat around the corner of the building against a concrete wall. Except for the graffiti on the wall and a modern-looking sign on the corner above the building, it looked just like the photo in the yellowed clipping.

Jennie pulled into the parking lot and went inside. A ceiling fan circulated stale but cool air around the store. The market with its scarred wooden floors had been updated with new soft drink fountains and a deli case. It was cluttered but clean and smelled like lemons. Jennie wondered if Annie's mother had come in here. Or had she lived in the neighborhood? Had she simply driven around town and randomly chosen that particular trash bin as she drove by?

# 17

"Can I help you, miss?" A woman with coarse gray hair and granny glasses perched on the end of her nose sat on a stool behind the counter. She pulled up a long strand of pale pink yarn from a full skein and continued to knit.

Thinking she'd get better cooperation if she bought something, Jennie said, "I'd like to get a drink."

"Help yourself. Everything's on the counter." The woman pointed toward the drink machine and kept working.

"Thanks."

Jennie filled her cup with ice and added some Coke.

"You live around here?" the woman asked.

"No, I go to school at Trinity High. We're temporarily in a warehouse on Delta Street. I'm Jennie McGrady."

"Nice to meet you, Jennie. I'm Gladys Swenson." She tipped her head down and eyed Jennie with a curious gaze. "Jennie . . . of course. Thought you looked familiar. Saw you on TV last night." She nodded approval.

"Oh. Then you know I sometimes do a little detective work."

"Detective work, huh? You want to question me about something? You maybe trying to find the hoodlums responsible for all the graffiti?" She made a clucking sound. "Terrible the way kids around here think they have to vandalize every building with a blank wall."

"I'm sorry, but that's not why I'm here." Jennie cleared her throat and dug into her backpack for her wallet, then set the clipping on the counter. After paying the woman, she showed her the old newspaper article. "I'm trying to find the store in this photo, and from the description in the paper, it looks like this one."

The woman set her knitting on her lap, adjusted her glasses, and glanced at the picture. "This is the store all right. I'll never forget that night. Police swarming all over the place looking for evidence and wanting to know if I knew anything about the baby. ''Course not,' I said. 'If I'd known about it, do you think I'd have left the poor thing in the trash?' "

Jennie took a sip of her Coke to hide her excitement. "The baby who was found that night is a good friend of mine. Her name is Annie Phillips. She's sixteen now."

"I heard she was adopted by a nice young doctor and his wife."

"Yes. Annie wants to find her birth mother. She asked me to help her. So that's why I'm here."

"Now, why would she want to find a mother that didn't want her? Probably still doesn't or she'd have made contact herself."

"I agree completely, but Annie's so upset. I think she just needs to know."

"Oh, sweetie, it was a long time ago. Trail's as cold as the Yukon in December."

"I know, but I have to try. Do you remember anything about that night?"

"Like it was yesterday."

"I suppose the police asked you if you'd seen anyone near the store that night close to when the phone call was made."

"Yep. I'll tell you the same thing I told them. I saw a woman in that phone booth right over there on the corner." She pointed to the phone in question.

From her perch near the door, Gladys had a good view of it.

"Billy and me both saw her. Billy—he's my husband—died last year. Billy said at the time it seemed strange to see a woman alone that time of night. He said he was going out to check on her, but by the time he got his coat on she was gone."

"Did you see a car?"

"Nope. She just disappeared into the night."

"Do you remember what she looked like?"

"Couldn't see her face because it was all in shadows. All we had were the streetlights. She didn't close the door on the booth. Apparently didn't want the light coming on. Still, I could see her fairly well. She was about my height—five four maybe. Wearing a white scarf over her head. She kept her back to the store the whole time she was in there, which wasn't more than a couple minutes. Had on one of those camel wool overcoats and white shoes. You know, I never did believe she was that baby's mother."

"Really?"

"This woman was a mite too spry for someone who'd just given birth. But who was I to say? Police figured it must have been the mother who called. I wasn't about to argue with them. Maybe the woman who used the pay phone didn't have anything to do with the baby. Might have been a coincidence."

"You really think she just happened to be there at the same time?" Jennie asked.

"No. I don't believe much in coincidences. The woman in that phone booth right out there—not a hundred feet from the trash where that baby was—called at the same time as 9-1-1 got the call about the baby. No, I didn't think it was a coincidence, but the police never asked me what I thought. They just wanted the facts."

Jennie tucked the clipping back in the envelope and stuffed it into her bag. "You mentioned she was too spry to be the baby's mother. What do you mean?"

Gladys gave Jennie a knowing smile. "You ever watch a woman walk right after she's given birth? Now, I know historically we've been told that some women used to just squat and deliver right out in the fields and go back to work like nothing happened. Having had six children, I find that hard to believe." She shook her head. "Trust me, a woman who has just had a baby wouldn't have been moving that fast."

"Maybe Annie's mother didn't throw her away. Maybe it was a friend or something."

"That would have been my guess. Still, it's hard for me to imagine anyone with a heart black enough to get rid of a baby like that."

"Maybe someone took the baby away from the mother," Jennie murmured to herself more than to Gladys.

"Honey, if someone had taken that sweet child from her mother, I can guarantee she wouldn't have ended up in the trash. That baby would most likely have been sold on the black market."

"Black market?" Jennie pulled a napkin from the container on the counter and wrapped it around her drink to absorb the moisture forming on the outside of her cup.

"Baby stealing. Done all the time. Someone takes a baby and sells it to people who are willing to bypass the regular channels and not ask questions."

Jennie shuddered. "That's awful. But I see what you mean. If a person was going to take Annie, they wouldn't just throw her away. They'd sell her. So if this woman wasn't Annie's mother, who was she?"

"The police never could figure that one out."

"The paper said she called in to say she'd heard the baby crying."

"Humph. I don't believe that for a minute. Think about it. If you walked by a trash bin and heard a baby crying, what would you do?"

"Investigate."

"Exactly. I'd have picked that baby up and gone into the nearest shelter."

"Which would be this store," Jennie finished.

"Right. You wouldn't be thinking of anything except saving that baby's life and getting her to safety as quickly as possible."

"Unless you were guilty of something—or maybe didn't want anyone connecting you with the baby."

Gladys sighed. "Don't think I haven't wracked my brain over this, honey, because I have. Nothing about it makes any sense whatsoever."

"Do you think the woman lived around here to have disappeared so quickly?"

"Maybe—hard to say. I didn't see or hear a car, but then, she might have parked a ways away so no one would be able to identify it. Police talked to all the residents but didn't come up with anything."

"I suppose a lot has changed around here since then. I was thinking about walking around the area to get a feel for it. See if anything—you know—strikes a chord."

"I suspect most of the people have moved out of the apartments. Except for being more run down, it's the same now as it was then. Same offices, same apartments. Only thing different is that the family planning clinic down the street was blown up a few days ago by some nasty anti-abortion protesters. All you'll see there is a pile of rubble. Don't know when the city plans to clean it up. Maybe they won't. Maybe someone could build something new—anything would be better for business than that eyesore. Not another abortion clinic. I don't much like living near a place like that. No telling what those protesters will do."

Jennie nodded. "On both sides."

"Hmm. You talking about that serial killer who's been gunning down the pro-lifers?"

"Yeah."

"Humph. Sad state of affairs when you can't even speak your mind on this issue or that. Intolerance, that's what it is."

"They caught one of the killers last night." Jennie told her about the killer calling her father to say he hadn't broken into Debra Noble's place or killed the last woman.

"The last one—that would have been Noreen Smith."

Jennie's eyebrows shot up. "You knew her?"

"Not well. Years ago she used to come into the store nearly every day to get a soft drink and a snack. She worked at that clinic around the corner." Gladys put a hand to her lips. "Glory be—I don't know why I didn't think about it before. Noreen stopped coming into the store 'bout the same time that baby was found."

"You think there might be a connection?"

"I couldn't say. It does seem an odd coincidence, though, doesn't it?"

Jennie sipped on her drink, a frown etching her forehead. "The white shoes . . . were they like nursing shoes?"

"I suppose they could've been. Didn't get a real good look at them."

"Could Noreen have been the woman you saw making the call?"

"I suppose it's possible, but it doesn't seem likely. The clinic wasn't open at night. Besides, they don't need to use our trash bin. They have their own way of disposing of the remains."

Jennie grimaced at the horrible thought. "I've heard that sometimes aborted babies live. Maybe Annie was aborted and lived." Jennie's mind raced with possibilities. The one foremost in her mind was Debra Noble's aborted baby. "Maybe Noreen Smith was assisting in a late-term abortion and saw the baby was alive. Rather than let it die, she put it in the trash bin and called the police."

Gladys shook her head. "That doesn't seem likely. Being a nurse, she'd probably take the baby to the hospital. I think that's what Noreen would have done. She was a nice lady."

"Gladys, I don't remember reading anything in the articles about those white shoes. That's a pretty important clue. Did you include those in your description of the caller?"

She narrowed her eyes and peered over the rims of her glasses. "I'm sure I did. I must have. 'Course, it could have slipped my mind—or I might not have thought about it until later—things like that happen. I remember being scared at the time. Worried the police might think Billy or I had something to do with it."

She took her glasses off. "I guess you'd have to get a look at the police files to know for sure."

"That's a good idea." Jennie doubted the police knew about the white shoes. If they had, wouldn't they have put two and two together and considered the fact that the baby might have come from the clinic? True, Annie had been found at night, but suppose the abortion had been performed after hours for some reason?

Of course, maybe the police had considered that possibility. Maybe they'd looked into the matter and hit a dead end.

Jennie felt like she had picked up a puzzle piece that didn't belong and no amount of maneuvering was going to make it fit.

Even if Noreen Smith had been the woman making the call, Jennie had no business thinking the baby might have been Debra's. "Well, I should go. I really appreciate your help."

"No problem. Come back and talk to me anytime." As Jennie opened the door, Gladys said, "If you find out anything, you be sure to let me know."

"I will."

Jennie drove slowly around the block, past rows of apartments that looked like they should have been torn down years ago. Turning the corner, the apartment complex continued. These looked better—as though someone had come in and remodeled them. At the next corner, Jennie hung another left. A tall chain link fence stood around the remains of a bombed-out building. Oddly enough, the sign identifying it sat out front. *Marsh Street Clinic*. It sat at the opposite corner from Mrs. Swenson's store. The alley behind it gave people going to the store from the clinic a straight shot. Noreen Smith had walked from here to the store lots of times, but she stopped coming after the baby was found. Now Noreen Smith was dead. Debra Noble had had an abortion sixteen years ago. Her house had been broken into last night. Annie had been placed in a trash bin after her birth.

The information Jennie had gathered jumbled around in her brain. Had Noreen Smith been the one Gladys saw that night? Had she been the woman who called 9-1-1? Had she merely heard the baby cry and reported it—or had she put the baby there? If so, why? Why throw a baby away when people would pay huge sums of money to buy her?

Jennie tried to imagine the scenario, but there were too many holes. Too many unanswered questions. She needed to talk to Debra to find out more details about the abortion. Where she'd had it and when, how far along she was, and the name of the attending physician.

A car honked behind her, and Jennie realized she'd stopped in the middle of the street. She pulled off to the side to let the car pass, then moved on herself. She'd finish her turn around the block, then go to the pool. Coach Dayton would not appreciate her being late again.

She approached the store from the side. As she'd noted earlier, the Dumpster was along the side wall near the alley. A gravel parking area lay between the sidewalk and the side of the building. Jennie pulled to a stop at the curb and walked across the parking lot. Stopping in front of the trash bin, she imagined herself carrying a small bundle. According to the newspaper articles, the bin had been nearly full.

What could have motivated a person to place a baby in a smelly garbage heap? Had the person thought the baby dead? Then why alert the authorities? Jennie shook her head to clear her mind. She started to walk away when she heard a scraping sound coming from inside the Dumpster. Jennie swallowed hard and walked back to it. She took a deep breath and grasped the handle, laying back the fold-in-half lid, then peered inside.

Tears stung her eyes. A sob stuck in her throat, and all she could manage was a whimper. "Oh, Annie."

# 18

Annie looked up at Jennie from the bottom of the smelly, empty Dumpster. She sat all curled up with her arms wrapped tightly around her legs. Her blue eyes were full of so much pain, Jennie had to look away.

"What are you doing here?"

Annie wiped the tears from her cheeks with a torn sleeve, leaving a wide black smudge. "I . . . I had to know what it was like. I went to see Gloria at school today. She said it might help me if I imagined myself as a tiny baby being put here by someone who cared about me. Someone who cared enough to call the police."

"She told you to come here?" Gloria was a counselor for the church and school. Jennie had seen her a few times herself.

"No. She had me do that in her office."

"Then why are you here?"

"I'm not sure. Gloria said I should imagine angels watching over me—protecting me and making sure someone came to save me. She said if I could see God holding me and loving me through it all, it would help me heal."

"Has it?"

"I'm not sure." Annie stood up, and Jennie helped her climb out. With her torn and dirty white blouse, mussed hair, and smudged face, she looked like a street urchin from *Oliver Twist*.

"Come on," Jennie said. "I'll give you a ride home."

"No. I . . . I can't go home like this. They'd want to know where I've been and I . . ." She closed her eyes. "I don't know what to tell them."

*The truth might be good.* Jennie didn't voice her opinion. It wasn't her place to tell Annie what to do. After all, maybe Annie's parents weren't as easy to talk to as hers were. And Jennie couldn't help but wonder if she might feel the same way if she were in Annie's situation. She settled an arm around Annie's slumped shoulders. "You can clean up at my place. I'm sure I have something that'll fit you."

Annie thanked her, and after waiting for Jennie to unlock the passenger side door, she slid onto the black vinyl seat. The car would definitely need cleaning now. Jennie rolled down the window. "No offense, Annie, but you smell pretty ripe. How long have you been in there, anyway?"

She shrugged. "A couple of hours."

After a long silence she spoke again. "Jennie, you'll probably think I'm stupid for saying this, but . . . I don't think my mother put me in there."

"Why?"

"Because . . ." She sighed. "I don't know. The papers said the police think she did it. But sitting in there like that, I had a lot of time to think. Maybe it's just wishful thinking, but there's something—maybe it's God—telling me she didn't do it. I don't expect anyone to understand. . . ."

"I think I do—at least a little," Jennie said. Though Jennie hadn't been adopted or abandoned in a trash bin, she knew what it was like to believe in something with your whole heart—even when all the evidence said otherwise.

"What do you mean?"

Jennie took a deep breath. "Well, it wasn't what you're going through, but in a way it's similar. Five and a half years ago a couple federal agents came to our door and said my father had been in a plane crash. They figured the plane had gone down in Puget Sound. Neither the plane nor the body was ever recovered."

"But your dad is alive."

"Yes. He wasn't killed in the crash." Jennie hesitated. So far the family hadn't told anyone the details of her dad's disappearance or that he'd been an undercover agent. Dad didn't seem to think secrecy mattered that much anymore. Still . . . "I'd appreciate it if you wouldn't say anything about what I'm going to tell you."

"I won't."

"Well, it was all an elaborate plan to make his enemies think he was dead. He needed to change his identity to protect him and us from drug dealers in South America. The thing is, I never once believed he was dead. Mom accused me of hanging on to a dream. Gloria said I needed to grieve and move on. They didn't understand why I kept insisting he was alive, but I knew in my heart he was."

"And you were right."

"Yeah." She gave Annie a tight smile. "I was so sure, I decided to try to find him. I almost got him and me killed in the process, but I found him."

"Oh, Jennie, you do understand." Annie tipped her head to one side. "How did you know I was in the Dumpster?"

"I didn't." Jennie explained her mission and told her about the conversation she'd had with Gladys. She carefully avoided any mention of Debra Noble's abortion because she didn't want to get Annie's hopes up. Just because Jennie had connected the two incidents in her head didn't make them so. "Gladys doesn't think the woman she saw that night could have just had a baby. If that's true, then you're right. Your mother didn't put you in that trash bin. It was the lady with the tan coat and the white shoes."

"White shoes," Annie mused. "I don't remember reading about that in any of the articles."

"I didn't either. Gladys says it may have been something she remembered later."

Annie frowned. "Do you think that nurse, Noreen Smith, did it?"

"I don't know—it could have been one of the other nurses working there. Or it may not have been a nurse at all."

"But if she did put me in the trash bin, and if she worked at the clinic, then—" Tears filled her eyes. "Oh, Jennie, then it's worse than I thought. My mother aborted me—she wanted me dead."

"No," Jennie insisted. "You're jumping to conclusions. We don't know anything for sure."

"You're right." Annie took a deep breath. "I need to stop worrying about it."

Annie leaned back against the seat and closed her eyes. Jennie chided herself for saying anything. She should have kept her mouth shut until she had more information. Annie felt bad enough thinking she'd been dumped and rescued.

---

By the time Annie had showered and changed into clean clothes, Jennie was already late for swim practice. Annie insisted she go to the pool and take her home later. Her parents wouldn't be expecting her until after practice anyway.

"Haul your carcass in here, McGrady," DeeDee yelled when Jennie walked through the door. "What do you think I'm running here—a tea party? Part of being an athlete is gaining a sense of responsibility. When you agreed to be on the team, you took on certain obligations. You can't just waltz in any time you feel like it. The team is depending on you. There are rules. You *did* read the rules, didn't you?"

"Yes, and I'm sorry. I—"

"Are you sick?"

"N-no."

"Are you dying?"

"No."

"Is someone in your family dying?"

"No . . . but—"

"Then I don't want to hear about it. I'm going to tell you this once and once only. Being late is an infraction of the rules. If you're late again, you are on the bench for the next meet. The next time, you're off the team. Do I make myself clear?"

"Yes, ma'am." Jennie pinched her lips together. She had done nothing wrong and wouldn't have been late at all if she hadn't stopped to help Annie. She didn't like being yelled at and was tempted to quit right then and there. But she had made a commitment to the team and to Coach Dayton.

"Then go suit up."

Jennie started to leave when Coach Dayton called her back. "You've never been in competitive sports before, have you, Jennie?"

"No."

"It isn't easy. I know you're thinking right now that it would be easier to just quit. That you don't need the hassle." She picked up a pencil and tapped it against her hand. "I hope you won't do that, Jennie. You've got talent, and I'd really like to see you stay in the sport."

Jennie smiled. "I won't quit."

"Good girl. Now, go get 'em."

For the next two hours, Jennie almost managed to put Annie and her troubles in a distant corner of her mind while concentrating on improving her swimming techniques. Heading home at six-fifteen, she felt dishrag limp and could hardly keep her eyes open.

---

"It's too much for her," Jennie heard her mother say. Mom's voice sounded far away.

"I don't think so." That was Dad. "She's still tired from my taking her with me the other night. I probably shouldn't have done that."

"There's more to it than that. She's not used to all this extra work with being on the swim team and my being pregnant. I just think it's too much."

"You think she should quit the team?"

"No . . . oh, I'm not sure, honey. What do you think?"

They were talking in lower tones now, and Jennie had to strain to hear them. She opened one eye. The room was dark. She'd fallen asleep again, only this time she hadn't even eaten dinner first. Her stomach rumbled in protest. She'd taken her books upstairs and fallen on her bed and hadn't moved since.

Should she let them know she was awake or play possum? The last thing Jennie needed this evening was a lecture on how she was trying to do too much. Mom had a point, but Jennie hated to admit it. Maybe she should let something go, but what? Certainly not her studies—though if she kept falling asleep instead of studying, her grades would soon plummet. She couldn't give up swimming—she'd promised to stick it out. And how could she not help Annie? Jennie knew perfectly well the exhaustion she felt every night was from more than the physical exertion of swimming. She was emotionally drained as well, weary from thinking and getting nowhere. She stretched and yawned. "Mom? Dad? What are you doing in my room?"

"I thought I'd better get you up to eat something." Mom moved closer to Jennie's bed.

"I know—it's the swimming. But don't worry, I'll get used to it."

"I think we'd probably better have you work out a schedule. A nap after dinner isn't a bad thing. Say, for twenty minutes— that's supposed to do the most good. Then you can do your homework. I'd like to see you in bed by nine-thirty on school nights with lights out by ten. That will give you a half hour to relax and read."

Jennie yawned and nodded. "Sounds okay to me."

Mom looked surprised that she'd given in without an argument. "Good. I'll dish up your dinner."

She eased around Dad, giving him a tender kiss. "Do you want to eat your dessert while Jennie's having her dinner?"

Dad grinned down at her and dusted her cheek with his finger. "Perfect, but only if you'll join us."

She batted his hand away. "Wouldn't miss it."

Jennie's heart did a little tumble like it always did when her mom and dad showed affection like that. She reveled in the fact that they still loved each other and had gotten back together. While Dad was missing, Mom had filed for a divorce so she could get on with her life. If Dad hadn't come back when he had, Mom would have married another man. Michael Rhodes was a great guy, but . . . No. She wouldn't think about that. It didn't happen. Her parents were working out their differences and seemed happier now than they'd ever been.

Mom left and Dad started to follow.

"Dad?"

He turned back to her. "Yeah?"

"I need to talk to you about something."

He came over and sat on her bed. "Shoot."

"Can you get me a copy of some police files on a case that happened sixteen years ago and was never solved?"

He arched an eyebrow. "Police files are confidential, Jennie. You know that."

"Yes, but I thought maybe if I came to your office, you could get it and . . ."

"What are you looking for?"

Jennie told him. "Um . . . Annie wants to find her birth mother."

"And she wants you to help her?"

"Right."

"Princess, I hate to disillusion you, but if the police couldn't find her right after if happened, do you really believe you have a chance now?"

"I didn't think so, but now I'm not so sure. I know the police thought Annie's mother was the person who put Annie in that trash bin and called them."

"But you don't?"

Jennie eyed him warily, not sure if he really wanted her opinion on the case or not. She decided to give it to him anyway. "Well, today I went to the neighborhood where she was found." Jennie squared her shoulders, half expecting him to yell at her.

He just stood there, waiting, arms folded. "Dad, it was the same store, and the lady there had seen a woman use the pay phone."

When her father still didn't comment, Jennie told him everything. "I need the police report to see if Gladys told them about the white shoes. I think it could be really important to the case. There might also be a connection with what's happening right now. I mean, Noreen Smith is dead, and Debra Noble could have been. Debra had an abortion sixteen years ago. I can't help but think—"

"Whoa." Dad slipped an arm around Jennie's shoulders. "That's quite a jump. Even if this woman in the white shoes was Noreen Smith, and even if she did place Annie in that Dumpster, to tie it in with Debra Noble is pretty farfetched."

Jennie's shoulders sagged. "I know. It's just that Annie looks so much like Debra and . . ." She sighed. "But you're right, I need to talk to Debra. Is she still here?"

"She's at work. She called your mother a few minutes ago and said she'd be here around ten. I guess she's staying here tonight, then will go to her apartment tomorrow."

"She's not alone, is she?"

Dad smiled. "No, princess, she's not alone. We've assigned an officer to follow her from the office to our place."

"Good. Anyone I know?"

"As a matter of fact, it is. Officer Rockwell has been assigned to her. She requested him."

Jennie felt an odd twinge of jealousy and wasn't sure why. "Can she do that?"

"She did. Appears she and the chief are good friends."

"Jason? Jennie?" Mom called from downstairs. "Are you coming?"

"Be right there, hon," Dad called.

"What about the file?" Jennie took his hand when he reached down to help her up.

"I'll take a look at it. I guess it won't hurt to tell you whether the white shoes got into the report. And you're right. It could be a crucial piece of information. As is the fact that the Smith woman used to work at the Marsh Street Clinic. You may have something there, Jennie. I'll see what I can find out tomorrow."

Over dinner Jennie asked her dad about the suspect they'd arrested the night before.

"I feel sorry for the man," Mom said. "With all he's been through, it's no wonder he snapped. Of course, murdering people isn't the answer."

"What happened to him?" Jennie sliced into a thick piece of roast beef.

"Apparently he's had a lot of mental problems—" Dad took a sip of his coffee—"but he seemed to be doing okay until recently when his wife gave birth to a severely handicapped child. The baby died after a couple months, and his wife left him. They had no insurance, and he ended up $600,000 in debt."

"So he just started killing people?" Jennie asked.

"Not exactly. In the early months of his wife's pregnancy, her gynecologist told her there was a strong chance the baby would be handicapped and said she should consider an abortion. She went to a crisis pregnancy center, and they talked her out of it."

"So he was out for revenge."

"In the worst way. We found a list in his room that included twenty women who worked at the various crisis pregnancy centers in the area. He claims he killed only two of them. Debra Noble and Noreen Smith were on that list, but he insists he hadn't gotten to them yet."

"Do you believe him?"

Dad took a bite of his apple pie and nodded. After swallowing he said, "Yes, I do. Noreen was tenth on his list. Debra was near the bottom. Forensics tells me the first two notes were written by someone wearing cotton gloves. We found those in his apartment. The last two notes had no cotton fibers."

"So there's another killer out there."

"I suspect so, which makes what you told me rather interesting. We'd been looking into the Smith woman's history, but I had no idea she used to assist with abortions. You do good work, princess."

Jennie's heart swelled with a sense of pride.

Mom looked from one to the other. "Okay, you two. No fair keeping secrets from me. What have you been up to now, Jennie?"

Dad filled her in while Jennie ate.

Mom looked thoughtful. "How did you know about Debra's abortion, Jennie?"

"She told me the other day, before my interview. See, I knew she'd been following Annie. She told Rocky she wasn't, but I could tell she was lying. When I confronted her, she broke down and told me about the baby she'd lost."

Mom sighed. "She told me about it too. Such a sad thing. I gave her the name of a woman who runs the support group at Trinity for women who have had abortions."

"Mom, did Debra say how far along she was when she had the abortion?"

"No, she didn't."

Jennie sliced into a large piece of broccoli, cutting off a tiny piece and coating it with a scoop of mashed potatoes and gravy to cover the taste. Broccoli was not her favorite vegetable, and she usually managed a bite small enough to swallow without too much chewing. After washing it down with a swig of milk, she said, "I don't suppose she said which clinic either."

"I'm afraid not, Jennie," Mom switched into her warning voice. "I think it would be best not to talk to her about it. If she brings it up, okay, but this is a very difficult time for her."

"But what if she's . . ."

Dad's cell phone rang, and Jennie's question died on her lips. The phone was reserved for police business and emergencies.

"McGrady here," Dad answered. His frown deepened. He muttered something under his breath and pushed his chair back. "I'm on my way." He folded the phone and put it back in the holder at his waist.

"What is it, Jason?" Mom asked. "What's wrong?"

"Debra and Rocky have been shot."

# 19

Jennie felt as though she'd been hit in the stomach with a cannonball. "Oh no. Are they. . . ?"

"They're both alive, thank God. An ambulance is taking them to the hospital. I have to go." Dad kissed them both and headed for the door.

Jennie wiped her mouth and tossed her napkin on the table. "I'm coming with you."

"No!" Mom and Dad yelled at the same time.

"Please. Rocky's my friend. And Debra doesn't have anyone."

Mom and Dad looked at each other with their what-are-we-going-to-do-with-her look. They were weakening.

"Please," Jennie pleaded again.

"All right," Mom said. "If it's okay with your father." To Dad she said, "She has a point. I'd go myself, but I don't feel up to it."

Dad caved. "Come on, then. But you'll have to do exactly what I say." To Susan he said, "We shouldn't be gone much more than an hour—two at the most."

*Yes!* Jennie grabbed a jacket from the hall closet and hurried out the door. Once in the car, she glanced at his stern, worried features. "They're going to be okay, aren't they?"

"I don't know, Jennie. I really don't know."

She closed her eyes and asked God to take care of both Rocky and Debra. Dad drove downtown and pulled in behind two double-parked police cars. They'd barricaded off a section of the street in front of the Channel 22 building. The scene looked much like the one in front of Debra's house last night.

Her father stepped out of the car. "Stay here, Jennie. I'm not sure what we're walking into, and I don't want you hurt."

Jennie started to object, then thought better of it. If she expected to go with him like this, she'd need to be on her best behavior. Dad could have said no, and she really did want to see Rocky and Debra. She slumped down in the seat and watched a hunched old man limp past the car. His gaze caught hers briefly, and the hairs on the back of her neck stood on end. He looked away and hurried past.

Jennie shivered and checked to make sure the doors were locked. Downtown Portland had its share of vagrants. Fortunately, this one seemed as frightened of her as she was of him. She shifted her attention to her father and rolled down the window a couple of inches so she could hear what was going on. Dad walked up to a uniformed officer and asked for a report.

"Witnesses said they heard one shot," Jennie heard the officer say. "But both Ms. Noble and Officer Rockwell were injured. Rock took the brunt of it."

Jennie gulped back a sob. Rocky had been seriously injured. Why couldn't Dad hurry? She wanted to get to the hospital.

"Anyone see the shooter?" her father asked.

"Not as far as we can tell. Several people heard the shot, but no one claims to have seen anything. It appears to have come from one of the apartments across the street—maybe the roof. I sent a couple of officers over there to have a look."

Dad nodded. "Who called it in?"

"Secretary inside the building said she heard the gunfire and called us right away. Says she didn't see anyone."

Jennie glanced at the five-story brick building on the other side of the street. At street level the structure housed a restaurant and an art gallery. Above that were apartments. The shooter would be long gone by now. One thing's for certain, it wasn't the psycho Dad had busted last night. He'd taken responsibility for the first two killings, but not Noreen Smith's. He also claimed he hadn't broken into Debra's apartment. So they were definitely looking for a second killer—maybe more. Had the shooter tonight been same person who'd broken into Debra's home? Was it the same person who killed Noreen Smith?

Dad and the officer went into the Channel 22 building. Jennie could hardly stand it. She wished she could get out of the car and start asking questions. Jennie looked at the building across the street again. In a lighted window on the third floor, she saw two police officers talking.

"The shot must have been fired from there," she murmured. "Whoever did it would have had a direct shot at anyone coming out the door."

Her dad walked in front of the car, blocking her view. Jennie unlocked the door. He opened the driver's side, but instead of getting in said, "We may have located the weapon and room the shooter used. The area's been secured. Would you like to come with me to check it out?"

"Sure. But what about Rocky?"

"He's in surgery right now. We won't be able to see him for a while. Debra's okay."

*Surgery.* "How bad is it?" Jennie asked when she joined him on the street.

"I don't know."

"You mean he might not make it?"

"There's always that chance." He hugged her to him. "Hey, I know you're concerned. So am I, but there really isn't much we can do now except pray he pulls through."

Jennie nodded. The lump in her throat made it impossible to speak. They crossed the street together, and Jennie offered up a silent prayer. She needed to pull herself together. Maybe she could even help track down the killer. Someone wanted Debra dead. But why?

The lobby of the brick building had been remodeled and still smelled of paint. It had a green marble floor that had been polished to a high-gloss shine.

A police officer greeted them as they entered and ushered them to a bank of three elevators. Dad introduced him as Sergeant Blake. The officer was tall, about Dad's height, and well built. His thick upper body reminded Jennie of a weight lifter's. Even without his bulletproof vest he'd have been big.

"What have we got?" Jason McGrady asked.

Blake scratched his blond head. "If the weapon hadn't been

left behind, and if the guy had hit his target, I'd have said it was a professional hit. The manager says he rented the room out this morning to an elderly man who said he wouldn't be moving in until next week."

"Name?"

"John Weed. Doesn't sound like he's the guy we're after, but we're having an officer check him out. According to the manager, this guy was pretty crippled up and half blind."

"Could be a disguise."

"That's possible."

"Is there a security guard in the building?"

"No. The building manager doesn't lock the doors until eleven—that's when the restaurant closes." The officer held the elevator door open while Jennie and her father stepped out. "Whoever used the room had a key."

Officer Blake led them to room 306. The door was open. The small one-bedroom apartment stood empty. It had been freshly painted and had a sterile feel to it. A faint sulphur smell hung in the air, attesting to the fact that a gun had recently been fired. An officer was working on the windowsill, dusting for fingerprints. A rifle lay on the beige carpet in front of the open window.

"Prints?" Dad asked.

"None so far." Blake hitched up his trousers and stepped inside. "Probably wearing gloves."

"Strange." Dad hunkered down to examine the weapon. "This is where he left it?"

"Yeah. Nothing's been moved."

Dad rubbed his chin and straightened. "What do you make of it, Jennie?"

"What?" Jennie did a double take. "Me?"

He grinned. "No one else here named Jennie."

"You actually want my opinion?" Jennie flushed as she caught Officer Blake's quizzical expression. He didn't comment.

"Wouldn't have asked if I didn't." To Blake Dad said, "Jennie's planning a career in law enforcement."

Jennie bit her lower lip, wishing she could come up with an intelligent response. "I'd guess it's the same guy who broke into Debra's place last night. He came to finish the job."

"Motive?"

Jennie shrugged. "She's a news anchor. Maybe she reported something bad about someone. Or maybe she knows something. Her house was ransacked. Could be the intruder from last night was looking for something. Um—evidence that might incriminate him, and he was afraid it would fall into the wrong hands." In the back of her mind, Jennie continued to make the connection between Debra and Noreen, but the only thing that seemed to link them together was that they were both pro-life and that one once helped doctors perform abortions and the other had had one. She almost mentioned it, then changed her mind.

"Good observations," Blake said. "Why do you think he'd leave the weapon in the middle of the room?"

She gazed at the rifle, trying to picture the man or woman leaving it on the floor. "Since there's no security guard, the shooter could have smuggled the gun into the building. A lot of people come and go. But once the shot was fired, people would be looking for the source of the gunfire. Maybe he dropped it and didn't have time to retrieve it." Jennie frowned. "Or got scared. Maybe he doesn't like guns and . . ."

"Why would you say that?" Blake asked.

Jennie stepped back and shrugged, feeling foolish. "Just an impression I got. I probably shouldn't have said anything—I mean, there isn't any evidence to suggest that."

Dad rubbed the back of his neck. "A lot of what we do is based on impressions, Jennie. I'm surprised he left the gun behind. This obviously wasn't a professional hit. The serial number may help us find out who bought it, but if it was purchased illegally, we're back to square one.

"I'm heading over to the hospital to question Ms. Noble," Dad told Blake. "Keep me posted. I'd like to know when you locate Mr. Weed."

"Will do, Lieutenant." Blake gave Jennie a warm smile. "Nice meeting you, Jennie."

Within minutes they arrived at the hospital. "I've got to check on Rocky first," Dad said. "You can go see Debra."

"I want to go with you. I need to see if Rocky is okay. And . . . I want to hear his version of what happened."

He hooked his arm around her neck and pulled her along. In the waiting room several reporters accosted them, wanting to know more about the late-breaking story. Dad gave his usual answer about it being an ongoing investigation, then squeezed through the crowd.

The emergency room was more chaotic than Jennie had ever seen it. Doctors, nurses, and other staff members wearing scrubs in an array of colors and prints bustled about. All of the dozen or so beds were occupied. They checked in at the nurses' station.

"I'm sorry. Officer Rockwell is still in surgery. There's a waiting room up there."

"Thank you. I'm aware of that." He flashed his badge and introduced himself. "I'm going to need to talk to him as soon as possible. Are you sure he isn't out of surgery yet?"

"I don't believe so. I'll check." After a brief phone conversation she hung up. "He's in recovery but is still sedated. The nurse said she'd let you know the minute he's alert enough to talk to you."

Dad pushed a hand through his hair. "What about Debra Noble?"

"Oh yes." The receptionist smiled. "She's in room 10."

"Thanks." Dad headed the direction she had pointed.

"Check with the nurse before you go in," the woman called after him.

Dad stopped to talk with one of the staff members, and seconds later they were standing beside the bed.

Debra's mascara-smudged eyes were closed. Her skin looked blanched and sallow against the white sheets. According to the nurse Dad had spoken with, Debra's injury wasn't serious. A bullet had grazed her right side.

"Ms. Noble." The nurse who stood on the opposite side of the bed hooked a stethoscope around her neck. "Detective McGrady is here. He'd like a few words with you."

Debra's eyes drifted open. She smiled. "Detective. How nice of you to come."

"I'd like to ask you a few questions."

"I suppose you want a blow-by-blow description." Her gaze shifted to Jennie. "Hi, Jennie. What are you doing here?"

"I wanted to make sure you were okay."

"That's sweet of you."

Dad cleared his throat. "Do you have any idea who the shooter might be?"

Debra's gaze drifted back to Dad. "I have no idea who shot at us. I didn't see anyone. I heard a shot, and Rocky threw himself against me. Knocked me to the ground." She winced. "He saved my life." Tears filled her eyes. She used the corner of the sheet to wipe them away, leaving a black mascara stain. "How is he?"

Dad rested his arms on the railing. "He's out of surgery—that's all I know."

Her blue eyes pooled again. "I've never known anyone who would risk their own life to save mine. It's unbelievable."

Jennie glanced at her father. She knew a lot of people willing to risk their lives for others. Dad was one of them. She was another—and Gram—and J.B. It was something you did out of love, duty, honor.

"Rockwell's a good man," Dad said.

"It's a God thing, isn't it?" Debra asked. "I mean, this concept of sacrificing one's life."

Dad looked uncomfortable. "My mother says it's evidence of God in us. I suspect she's right about that."

Debra sighed. "I think they're going to let me go home. Can I stay at your house again?"

"Of course," Dad said. "It might be a good idea if you stayed out of the limelight for a few days."

"Sure. As soon as I get cleaned up and give the station my story. I've got some vacation time coming."

"We'll wait for you to be discharged and give you a ride home."

"Thanks. I appreciate that. Is there anything new I can tell people about the investigation?"

Dad heaved a heavy sigh. "I wish there were, Ms. Noble."

Jennie looked up when she heard the tap of the receptionist's heels on the linoleum floor. "Detective McGrady, Officer Rockwell is awake and in his room. He's asking to speak with you."

# 20

Seeing Rocky so pale and helpless shook Jennie to the core. Rocky had taken a bullet in the back. It had torn through his stomach, then come out the other side and hit Debra. Besides his IV, which transported fluids and antibiotics into his veins, a tube protruded from his nose and went into a bottle that sat on top of a suction machine. A small green tube draped around his head, the two prongs providing oxygen directed into his nostrils.

She stood beside her father, praying with all her heart that Rocky would recover.

"Hey." Rocky tried to smile.

"Hey yourself, buddy." Dad leaned close to him. "Can you tell me anything about what happened out there?"

"Right . . . before the . . . shooting . . ." Rocky winced, then went on. "I spotted a guy . . . in the building. Window open. Brown coat. Saw reflection. Gunshot."

"Take it easy, Rocky. We found the weapon and the room he used. Did you see his face?"

Rocky shook his head. "Debra?"

"She's okay." Dad took hold of his hand. "You did good. Real good." To Jennie he said, "We'd better go, princess."

Jennie bit her bottom lip. "In a minute." When Dad stepped back, she moved to Rocky's side. He held his hand up and she grabbed it.

"Don't look so worried, kid."

"You're not going to die on me, are you?"

"Not a chance, McGrady." He squeezed her hand. "Not a chance."

A nurse came over to check on him and urged Jennie and her father to leave. Jennie complied, promising to visit the next day.

Dad wrapped an arm around her as the elevator carried them down to the main floor.

Jennie turned and put her arms around him. "I don't think I could stand it if Rocky died."

"He won't. You heard him." Dad's voice seemed strained. "There . . . there isn't anything going on between you two, is there? Something I should know about?"

"Dad . . ." Jennie moved away from him. "He's my friend." Jennie set her jaw, determined not to cry. Why did people always think that? Rocky meant a lot to her. She didn't understand why the bond between them was so strong. It just was. She didn't like thinking or talking about it. Sometimes she did wonder what it would be like if she were older or Rocky were younger, but that wasn't the case.

"I'm sorry, princess. It's just that when I left, you were only eleven. Now I come back and you've turned into a beautiful young woman. And you've got all these guys swarming around you. I'm not ready for you to be interested in a serious relationship—especially not with someone as old as Rockwell. He's a great guy, but—"

"Dad," Jennie sighed, "you don't need to worry."

He didn't look convinced. The elevator doors swished open. Jennie went to get Debra while Dad headed to the parking lot to get the car. He'd meet them out front.

Jennie didn't say much on the way home, just listened to Debra and Dad discuss Rocky's condition and who might want her dead. Dad asked her if there was anyone in particular she could think of who might want to hurt her.

"Not specifically. Being a reporter, I sometimes get emails or letters from people objecting to something I've said or a subject we've covered, but I can't think of anything that would cause someone to want to kill me."

"Do you have any connection at all with the woman who was murdered the other day—Noreen Smith?" Dad asked.

"When I first saw her picture, I thought she looked vaguely familiar, but I haven't been able to place her. I may have seen her at one of the crisis pregnancy centers. I understand she volunteers there." Debra tipped her head back against the seat. "If you don't mind, I'd just as soon not answer any more questions."

"Of course, I'm sorry."

"Don't apologize. I know you're just trying to do your job. Maybe I'll be able to think more clearly tomorrow. The pain medication they gave me seems to have turned my brain to mush."

Once they arrived home, Jennie left Debra in Mom and Dad's care and went to bed. She fell asleep asking God for answers and for Rocky's recovery.

---

"Do you always have to wait this long?" Jennie asked. She and her mother had been sitting in the doctor's office for an hour. As part of her project on fetal development, she wanted to include the importance of routine doctor visits. She also wanted to see firsthand what the doctor did during those visits and maybe listen to the heartbeat.

"Not always. It shouldn't be much longer." Mom set down a tattered copy of *Better Homes and Gardens* and picked up a stale issue of *House Beautiful*. "Dr. Ellison had a delivery this morning, so he's running behind.

"Hmm." Mom glanced at her watch. "In a way that's good. Your dad may make it after all."

Dad had called the doctor's office fifteen minutes earlier to see if Mom and Jennie were still there. He promised to meet them there as soon as he could.

"Susan McGrady," the nurse called. Jennie followed them through the reception area into a wide hallway, where Mom handed Jennie her purse, slipped off her shoes, and stepped on the scale.

"Hey, good job, Mom. You're up another five pounds."

Mom grinned and patted her belly. "Making up for lost time. I hope it slows down, though. I'll be a blimp if I keep gaining at this rate."

"I wouldn't worry about it," the nurse said. "You'll do fine."

Once they were in the exam room, Susan introduced Jennie

to the nurse and explained why she'd come. "Jennie, this is Marie Olson, Dr. Ellison's nurse."

"Hi, Jennie. Welcome. A fetal development project, huh? That's quite an undertaking. I have a booklet on prenatal care and a textbook on obstetric nursing that you can use for research." She pulled a blood pressure cuff out of a wire basket mounted on the wall. "Oh, and I'll bet Dr. Ellison would let you watch him deliver a baby if you'd like."

"Really?" Jennie sat on the edge of her chair. "That would be so cool. Mom says I can be with her when the baby is born, but my project is due before that."

"We'll ask him, okay?"

Jennie watched and made notes while Marie took Mom's blood pressure, pulse, and temperature and recorded them. To listen to the baby's heartbeat, Marie used a machine called a Doppler, which magnified the sounds in Mom's stomach. "I'm picking up a strong heartbeat." She looked at Jennie, then to Susan. "Can you hear it?"

Mom smiled. "Sure can."

Jennie had a hard time distinguishing between sounds but thought she picked up a faint, rapid beat. Her mouth stretched into a wide grin as she imagined what the baby would look like. According to her research, a twelve-week fetus would be pretty well formed. It would have discernible toes and fingers. A picture Jennie had seen showed one sucking its thumb. It was so cute.

After measuring Mom's stomach with a calibrator, she said, "You can get dressed. We won't need to do a pelvic exam today, Susan, but the doctor would like to talk with you."

"About the tests he did last week?"

"I assume so, yes."

Mom's smile faded. "Did he find something?"

"I can't really say. It's best if he talks to you about it."

*She can't say? That means there's a problem.* Jennie felt the joy drain out of her and slip into some dark hole. *Please, God,* she prayed. *Please let our baby be okay.*

Minutes later they sat side by side in twin chairs facing Dr. Ellison from across a wide, cluttered desk. He had several pictures—one of himself and Dr. Phillips holding golf clubs and a trophy. Another of Annie and one of Annie and her parents. His wall was nearly covered with assurances that he was not only an award-winning gynecologist but had received many accolades in research and community service.

When he came in, Mom told him about Jennie's project. He nodded in response, his attention clearly focused elsewhere.

"Marie said I might be able to watch you deliver a baby," Jennie said.

"Yes, I'm sure we can work something out." He cleared his throat, still preoccupied with the chart in front of him.

"Mrs. McGrady, Jennie." His solemn demeanor told Jennie the problem was serious. She hoped she was reading him wrong. "There may be a problem. I . . . um . . . I was hoping your husband would be with you today."

"He was—"

The office door opened. Dad poked his head in. "Sorry I'm late. Got here as quickly as I could."

"Come in, Mr. McGrady." Dr. Ellison took a folding chair from the corner and set it beside Mom's.

Mom looked up and gave her husband a wan smile.

Dad took her hand and sat down. "Is something wrong?"

"I'm afraid so." Dr. Ellison looked at the file on his desk, then slowly let his gaze slide from Dad to Jennie and finally to Mom. "As you know, Susan, we did several tests last week. We're not one hundred percent certain, but the test results show your baby may have Down's syndrome."

Jennie's hand tightened around her braid. A dull ache bore into her chest in the vicinity of her heart.

Mom fiddled with the straps of her handbag.

"Are you sure?" Dad covered Mom's hand with his.

"These tests are usually right, but there is always a slight chance the baby could be fine. I need to go over some alternatives with you."

"Alternatives? Are you going to suggest I have an abortion?" Mom asked.

*This can't be happening.* Jennie hardly dared to breathe. Her gaze passed from one to the other. She couldn't believe what she was hearing. *Mom wouldn't do that, would she?* Didn't children with Down's syndrome have just as much right to be born as anyone else? Weren't they just as important as other kids? Jennie had personally met only one child with Down's—Kathryn, a cute, bubbly little girl whose parents went to Trinity.

"No, of course not," Dr. Ellison said. "I'm not recommending anything at this point. But I am required to give you the information. Ultimately the choice will be yours."

Jennie swallowed past the lump in her throat. *Choice.*

"Of course," Mom said. "It always boils down to that, doesn't it? A woman's choice." She looked over at Dad as if she expected him to do something—to somehow turn back the clock and make the pain go away. "It's not my choice alone."

Dad squeezed Mom's hand but seemed as much at a loss for words as Jennie.

"I'll give you some information about Down's syndrome to read over," the doctor went on. "If you do choose to terminate the pregnancy, you'll want to have it done as quickly as possible. I'll need to refer you to another doctor. As you know, I don't perform abortions."

"Yes. I do know that. I'm surprised you would even mention it as an option." She met his gray blue gaze.

"I have to. Patients have a right to make informed choices."

"What if I decide not to abort the baby? Is there any way of knowing how severely handicapped the child will be?"

"I'm afraid not. Many women have opted to give birth to their Down's children and are happy they did. There are varying degrees of disability—retardation, a short life span. You may want to go to one of the support group meetings. They can give you an idea of what it's like to raise a child with Down's. I will say that many of these children do quite well. There is a wide range in their abilities."

"I . . . I'm aware of that." Mom stared at something on the wall behind Dr. Ellison's head. "I can't imagine aborting this baby. I don't understand why this is happening, but I do trust God to work it all for good."

"I feel the same way, honey. Regardless of the outcome, we'll manage. I think we should go ahead with the pregnancy."

His words seemed to revive her. Mom squared her shoulders and turned to look at Jennie. "How do you feel about this, Jennie?"

"I think you should keep the baby."

Mom smiled. "I would like to see the Down's literature, Dr. Ellison. But I'm not going to have an abortion, and I really don't think I want any more tests. It's better not knowing."

Dr. Ellison nodded and seemed relieved with their decision. "In some cases, I agree. On the other hand, there are problems that can be corrected in utero. But we can talk about that later. His gaze wandered to the picture of Annie. "I'm grateful that we've made so many advances. " He picked up the photo. "My granddaughter, Annie," he said proudly. "Being born prematurely, Annie wouldn't have made it back when I first started in medicine. There are pros and cons with everything.

"I'm sorry." He set the picture down. "Is there anything more I can help you with?"

"No. I'll see you next week." Mom gave him a tight smile and managed to get to the car before breaking down completely. Dad gathered her in his arms and held her.

"Jennie," Dad said, "why don't you go ahead. I'll take your mom home."

"Sure. Is it okay if I go by the hospital to see Rocky? I don't have to go to any classes today."

"That's fine," Mom said.

Jennie hugged her mom, holding back her own tears. "I'm glad you're going to have the baby. Nick and I will help. It'll be okay."

Mom nodded and crawled into Dad's car. Jennie slowly made her way across the parking lot to her own car, then remembered that Marie was going to give her research material for her project. Jennie hurried back inside, got the books, thanked Marie, and left.

As she pulled out into the street, she headed for the hospital. But fifteen minutes later, she drove into the parking lot of the Park Hill Clinic instead. She hadn't meant to stop there but had seen the sign, made a U-turn at the next light, and gone back.

It was one of those crazy things a person did without thinking. Now that she was there, Jennie didn't know why she had come or what she should do next.

"*Follow your hunches,*" Gram had often told her. "*Sometimes you need to go with your instincts rather than your head.*"

A dark green van sat at the curb in front of the clinic, its side door open. It seemed to serve as a pit stop of sorts for several protesters. At least a dozen picket signs leaned against the side. The words were painted in red: "Baby killers." "Abortion is murder." An older woman in a white blouse and black slacks sat on a folding chair in the shade of a midsize tree, drinking from a water bottle. She glared at Jennie. Jennie quickly looked away.

Two protesters carried signs and walked back and forth in front of the clinic. One of them, a clean-shaven man with a slight build, carried one of the baby-killer signs. The woman carried one that read "Stop the insanity." Another woman carried pamphlets. They were all watching Jennie as she left her car and walked toward the clinic.

"Abortion kills babies!" one of the women yelled.

"Murderer!" the man screamed at her.

Jennie stared at him in surprise. "I'm not . . ." She started to defend herself when he took a menacing step toward her. His hateful gaze bore into her. Jennie's words caught in her throat. Nervousness about going into the clinic melted into a consuming terror. She'd seen that look in only one other person—the neo-Nazi skinhead who had attempted to kill her only a few weeks before.

# 21

Jennie's feet froze to the concrete walk. Her heart hammered against the wall of her chest.

The woman with the pamphlets grabbed the man's arm. "Adam," she soothed, "you can't—" He shrugged away and glared at Jennie again but didn't come any closer.

"Don't kill your baby." The woman held one of her pamphlets out to Jennie. "There's a better way."

Anger welled up inside Jennie, easing out a portion of her fear. These people had already judged and condemned her, and she had done nothing but follow an urge to come to the clinic to ask some questions.

"Baby killer!" the man shouted again.

Even though he hadn't made a move toward her this time, Jennie stepped back. Maybe she should leave.

"Come in. Quickly," an urgent female voice called.

Jennie glanced toward the clinic. An attractive woman wearing a long, floral print dress and a white lab coat held open the door.

Jennie turned from the protesters and ran inside. When the door closed behind her, she began to breathe normally again.

The waiting room had only one other person in it besides Jennie and the woman who'd rescued her—a receptionist who sat behind a large desk, phone to her ear. She glanced briefly at Jennie, then began writing something on a yellow legal pad.

"I am so sorry," the woman said. She had shoulder-length permed hair and smelled of gardenias. The gold name pin on the pocket of her lab jacket read *E. Whitestone, R.N.* "Did they hurt you?"

"N-no. I'm fine." That wasn't quite the truth. The encounter had left her trembling.

E. Whitestone, R.N., sighed and shook her head. "We call the police almost every day. Unfortunately, they have a right to protest as long as they don't come onto our property."

"They're out here every day?"

"Almost. Oh, not the same people. They alternate, but . . ." She sighed again. "Usually there isn't a problem. Once in a while, though, we get radicals like the man out there today. His type worries me. He's volatile and . . . there are days I literally fear for my life."

"I can see why."

She smiled as though putting the traumatic moment out of her mind. "I'm Ellen Whitestone. What can I do for you?"

Jennie introduced herself. "I . . . I wanted to ask you some questions."

She gave her an understanding nod. "Certainly. Let's go back to my office. We can talk there."

Ellen was apparently under the same assumptions the protesters were. Jennie didn't bother to set her straight. That could wait. Jennie followed her down a hallway and settled into the chair in front of a desk. Instead of going around behind the desk, Ellen pulled a chair beside Jennie.

"Now," Ellen said, "how can I help you?"

"Like I said, I have some questions." Jennie sighed. "I should tell you, though, I'm not pregnant."

"I'm glad to hear that. Did you want to talk about birth control?"

"No," Jennie said quickly. "I'm into abstinence. See, I don't plan on having sex until I get married, and for me that's a long way off. I just want to ask you about the clinic that was bombed a few days ago."

"The Marsh Street Clinic?"

"Yeah."

A frown wrinkled the soft skin around Ellen's eyes. "What did you want to know?"

"I just wondered if you knew anyone who might have worked there about sixteen years ago."

Her frown deepened. "Sixteen years—that's a long time. Why do you ask?"

Jennie pulled a newspaper article out of her pack. "This woman was murdered last week. Her name is Noreen Smith. She used to work there."

Ellen studied the photo. "At the Marsh Street Clinic? There must be some mistake. This woman was a pro-life advocate. She wouldn't be working in a clinic like this."

"I think she did a long time ago. There may be a connection between this Noreen Smith's death and the bombing. The crimes were committed within a few of days of each other."

"Even so, the serial killer has been caught. I'm sure the police are . . ."

Her eyes narrowed again. "What is this? Are you with the police or something? You seem so young."

Jennie smiled. "Not yet, but I do hope to be in law enforcement someday."

Her eyes widened in recognition. "Wait a minute. I thought you looked familiar. You were on television the other night. Debra Noble interviewed you."

"Um . . . yeah. Look, I'm here because a friend of mine just found out she was a throw-away baby and asked me to help find her birth mom. According to the papers, Annie's mom threw her away, then called the police and told them where to find her."

"How sad for her. I can understand your wanting to help, but the chances of finding the birth mother seem pretty slim."

"I know." Jennie shrugged. "But see, I don't think her birth mom threw her away. I might have some new evidence in the case. I have a hunch this nurse"—Jennie pointed to the photo in the article—"put her in a Dumpster and called the police. I also have reason to believe she was working at the Marsh Street Clinic at the time. The trash bin is only a short distance away from the clinic. See, I think my friend's birth mother had an abortion and her baby survived."

She shook her head. "That's not possible. Most doctors won't do late-term abortions—especially on healthy fetuses. It would be extremely rare to have babies live through an abortion. Besides, if a baby does happen to survive, we would never throw it away. We'd do everything we could to save it."

Jennie pinched her lips together. "I'm trying to figure out what might have happened. I was hoping maybe I could find someone who worked at the Marsh Street Clinic—and who might have known Noreen."

"Well, we did have a nurse come in to apply for a job yesterday. She had been working there for the past seven years."

"Did you hire her?"

"No. Unfortunately, we don't have an opening right now."

"Who is she?"

"I'm sorry, Jennie, but I can't give you that information."

Jennie sighed. "I just want to ask her some questions. It's really important."

"I suppose I could give her a call. Wait here a minute." She stepped out of the office and closed the door behind her.

Jennie got up and walked to the window. The protesters were talking to a young girl—maybe high school age. She looked as frightened as Jennie had been. Jennie felt sorry for her. Something was very wrong with the picture framed by the window. Jennie didn't like the idea of women having abortions. She didn't like heavy-handed bullying by some of the anti-abortion protesters either. Intimidation was hardly the way to get a pregnant girl to change her mind.

*What would Jesus do?*

The question hung in her head unanswered as Ellen returned. "I may be able to help you after all. The gal we interviewed doesn't know Noreen, but she gave me the name of a woman who might." Ellen handed her a business card on which she'd written the name Lucy Bennett and a phone number.

Jennie thanked her and left, but instead of going straight to her car, she went out to the curb. The girl she'd seen earlier was inside the clinic now—away from her tormentors. Jennie's anger at the way the protesters had accosted them far exceeded any fear she'd felt earlier. She straightened and deliberately squared her shoulders, not stopping until she was face-to-face with the man who'd been so hateful. She was taller than he was by at least four inches.

Surprise glinted in his gray-green eyes.

"There's something you should know." Jennie hooked her fingers around the straps of her backpack.

He frowned and took a step back as if being too close to Jennie might contaminate him.

"I am not pregnant." Jennie stepped forward. "I have no intention of getting an abortion. And I have no intention of letting you or anyone else threaten me. What you are doing is wrong."

"I wasn't threatening anyone." He seemed less formidable now. "God hates abortion. It's wrong. We have to stop it."

"God hates divorce, too, so why aren't you out there picketing lawyers' offices?"

The man's face contorted in anger. "You're comparing the murder of innocent babies with . . . with divorce?"

"A sin is a sin. Isn't that what the Bible says?"

He raised his fist.

"Adam, don't—" The woman with the pamphlets put a restraining hand on his arm.

"Stay out of it, Claire." He pushed her aside.

"Go ahead and hit me." Jennie leaned toward him. "I'll have you put in jail so fast—"

She should have turned and run the other way. She didn't really think he'd do it. His fist shot out. Jennie raised her arm to ward off the blow, but he slammed her arm away and clipped her jaw. The force of his blow knocked her backward. Her foot caught on a crack in the sidewalk. She landed on her rear and was absolutely certain she'd never be able to get up.

By the time the pain settled down and she realized she'd walk again, a squad car had pulled up behind the van. Jennie struggled to her feet. A uniformed officer emerged. "What seems to be the problem here?"

"We called, officer." Ellen hurried down the walk toward them. "This man has been harassing our clients, and I just saw him assault this young girl as she was leaving our facility."

Jennie rubbed the sore spot on her arm. Adam looked stunned. The woman he'd called Claire was crying. The officer pulled out a pad and turned to Jennie. "Want to tell me what happened?"

"Please don't arrest him." Claire turned to Jennie. "We have six children and . . . an arrest could cost him his job."

Jennie rubbed her injured hip.

"The man's a menace," Ellen said. "He should be in jail."

"Oh, you'd like that, wouldn't you?" One of the other women set her picket sign down. "Well, Miss *Pro-choice*, you can put us in jail, but that won't stop us. Nothing will stop us until *you* put an end to this senseless killing."

"That's enough," the officer barked. Turning back to Jennie, he asked her name.

She gave it and told him what had happened. "All I wanted to do was tell him to back off a little. I could be wrong, but it seems to me that gentleness would work a lot better for them than intimidation."

Jennie looked at the red spot forming on her arm. It was the same one she'd broken a few months earlier. She hoped he hadn't rebroken it.

"Do you want to press charges?" the officer asked.

A moment ago she'd have cheerfully told the officer to throw the book at him. But that was before she heard about the children. *He's a menace*, part of her insisted. Another said, *He's misguided. He needs help.* She'd seen the way he'd pushed his wife away in anger. Did he abuse her in other ways as well?

"I guess I provoked him," she told the officer. "It was partially my fault. I shouldn't have confronted him. On the other hand, he shouldn't have hit me." Taking a deep breath, she said, "Yeah, I want to press charges."

While she watched the arrest process, Jennie wanted to take it back. She couldn't look at Adam or his wife. *You're doing the right thing*, she told herself.

Ellen expressed those thoughts aloud.

"I hope so," Jennie mumbled.

"Of course you are. We can't let these people get away with violence. We have to fight for our rights."

Jennie turned an annoyed gaze at her. "You think I did this to help your cause?"

"Of course. We all need to stand up against fundamentalists like this who want to take away our right to choose."

"I'm pro-life." Jennie watched Ellen's face transform from ally to enemy.

"Then why—"

"Violence is wrong, no matter who does it. I'm not having Adam arrested because he's pro-life or because he hit me. I'm hoping that through it he'll get the help he needs to deal with his temper. Adam has a right to protest. I just don't agree with his tactics."

Jennie looked around at the protesters who'd gone silent. She looked at the weeping wife and the angry Adam. Her gaze came back to Ellen, who obviously felt betrayed. In the past few minutes she'd alienated all of them. "Thanks again for the information," Jennie said to Ellen.

She spoke briefly to the police officer and agreed to go down to the station to file a formal complaint later that day. Walking back to her car, Jennie wondered when she'd have time. It was almost one, and she still wanted to see Rocky and do some homework before swimming. But she also wanted to pay a visit to the woman Ellen said might have known Noreen. No doubt about it, her life was getting far too complicated.

Jennie drove away from the clinic feeling as though she'd engaged in a major battle. She had confronted people in the past, but this was the first time she'd been so brazen about it. Well, maybe not. She remembered confronting the neo-Nazis who claimed to be Christians yet hated people whose skin color didn't match theirs.

Still, she couldn't help wondering if she'd gone too far in confronting the pro-life group. She probably shouldn't have gone to the clinic in the first place. Embarrassment coursed through her now as she thought about what she'd done. She gripped the steering wheel to keep her hands from shaking, but the move did little to stop the butterflies flitting around in her stomach.

She wondered what Mom and Dad would say. More important, she wondered what Gram would have done. Jennie imagined her saying, "You did the right thing, darling."

Had she really? Jennie felt good about getting the phone number from Ellen. A sense of uneasiness wrapped itself around her. Suppose Ellen had called the name on the card and told her Jennie was the enemy. Suppose the woman refused to talk to her. Jennie made a right at the next block into a service station and stopped in front of a phone booth.

She dug into her pocket for the card, deposited money into the pay phone, and dialed the number. The line was busy. Just as well. A face-to-face visit would be better anyway—especially if Ellen had called to warn her. Jennie flipped through the pages of the phone book. Lucy Bennett lived in Oregon City. Not far from where she was. She could easily stop there before going to the hospital.

Lucy Bennett's place was swarming with cops. An ambulance stood with its doors open while two EMTs placed a shrouded body inside.

# 22

Jennie's insides collapsed. At least that's what it felt like. *Pull yourself together, McGrady. It might not even be her.* "It is," she said aloud. "I know it is." Noreen and Lucy had worked in the same clinic. Jennie backed off on her runaway thoughts. Noreen hadn't worked there for sixteen years. It was too soon to make that kind of an assumption.

She found a parking spot a block away and walked back.

The officer apparently assigned to keep people away from the crime scene had his back to her and was occupied with a group of reporters. Jennie cut through the lawn and went up the stairs.

A strong hand grasped her arm from behind. "Sorry, miss, you can't go in there."

Jennie swung around. "I have to talk to the investigating officer. I'm Jennie McGrady and—"

Recognition lit his brown eyes. "Detective McGrady's kid?"

"Yeah. I'd like to see him."

Hands on hips, he maneuvered himself around to bar her way inside. "He isn't here."

"Maybe he should be. Lucy—"

"Lucy?"

"Yes—the woman who lives here."

"You know the victim?"

So it *was* her. "N-no . . . not exactly. How did she die? Was she murdered?"

"Don't think so, but it's too soon to tell. The medical examiner says it looks like a drug overdose."

152

Jennie brushed her bangs aside. "Somehow I don't think it's as simple as that."

He eyed her suspiciously. "Sounds like you know something. Maybe you'd better talk to Detective Mallory."

The detective came outside when Officer Dunn called him. After introducing her, he told Mallory that Jennie had come to visit the deceased.

Mallory, of course, wanted to know the entire story. Jennie obliged by first telling him about the connection she'd found between Noreen and Lucy. "Doesn't it seem strange to you that Noreen and Lucy used to work in the Marsh Street Clinic and now both of them are dead and the clinic's been bombed?"

Mallory frowned. "That's very interesting. I'll take your concerns under consideration. If it looks like they might be related, I'll talk to your dad. Speaking of which, I doubt he'll be too happy with you missing school to play detective."

"I'm part homeschooled and don't have classes today." She sighed, knowing she'd just hit another wall. There was no way she'd be able to get into Lucy's home or find out anything about what went on in the Marsh Street Clinic sixteen years ago. She was back to square one. She doubted Ellen would help her find someone else who might have worked there. "I don't suppose I could go in and look around?"

"Sorry. Look, Jennie, your dad told me you wanted to be a detective. But you're not one yet, and until you are—"

"I know. It's none of my business." Jennie peered inside the small cottage. "You'll talk to my dad about this?"

"I will." His gray gaze met hers head on. He wasn't angry, Jennie noticed, just concerned. "I'm sure you've heard this before, but it bears saying again. We do a pretty good job of catching criminals and solving crimes. I think we can manage this one without you as well." His expression sobered even more. "I wouldn't want to see you hurt."

"I'm not in any danger."

"Yes, you are. Think about it. If this Bennett woman was murdered, as you seem to think, it happened within the hour. If you'd come any sooner than you did, you may have been met by a killer instead of a cop."

Jennie swallowed hard. His comment smacked her between the eyes with the force of a two-by-four.

"Go back home, Jennie. Leave the investigating to the professionals."

Jennie mumbled something incoherent and jogged back to her car. She didn't want to think about Mallory's warnings, but they came back at her full force. If she'd come straight from the clinic instead of confronting the protesters, she might have come face-to-face with the person who killed Lucy and maybe Noreen—and who'd injured Rocky in his attempt to kill Debra. And who may have bombed the Marsh Street Clinic.

Jennie sucked in a deep breath. The crimes all had to be related. What she couldn't understand was how Debra fit into it. Someone was definitely out to get her. For the moment she was safe. Debra had the benefit of a police escort. They'd be even more wary now. Jennie doubted the killer would go after her again.

Did the killings and attempted murder have anything to do with Annie? *Don't forget about yourself, McGrady. Suppose the killer finds out you've been asking questions. You could be in danger too.* Jennie canceled the thought and drove straight to the hospital. Nothing was connecting as it should, and at the moment she had more important things to think about.

Rocky was asleep, but the nurse had told her his condition had been upgraded to good during the night. Jennie decided to sit with him for a few minutes, hoping he'd wake up while she was there. Opening her backpack, she pulled out a lined pad and began writing down the events of the last few days and her observations. She began a list of suspects but found it hard to come up with anyone viable. The man allegedly responsible for the first two pro-life murders was in jail. Charity had admitted to breaking into the journalism room and rewriting Gavin's article. While Charity had been cruel and hurtful, Jennie couldn't see her as a murderer.

Jennie wrote down Debra Noble under the suspect list and tapped her pen against the pad. She shook her head. Debra did not shoot at herself. She hurriedly scribbled down the names of people connected with Annie and Debra. Dr. and Mrs. Phillips.

Annie's grandparents. The people Jennie had met at the station during her interview with Debra. She even wrote down Gladys, the woman who owned the store and the Dumpster where Annie had been found. Gladys knew Noreen and may have known Lucy. Her store was near the Marsh Street Clinic. But, no, Gladys didn't strike Jennie as the sort who'd go around bombing abortion clinics or killing people. What reason would she have?

So far she was coming up with nothing. *Why even bother, McGrady? You're getting nowhere. You're not a cop. You don't have all the facts. You may as well give up.*

But she couldn't. Something niggled at the back of her mind—something important, but she couldn't quite reach it.

"Hey, Jen." Rocky's blue gaze met hers. "What are you working on?"

She smiled and tucked the pad away. No sense in upsetting him. And he would be upset. "Just making some notes. Nothing important." She scooted closer to the bed. "How are you feeling?"

He closed his eyes. "Like I've been shot."

"Very funny. You must be feeling better."

"If you say so." His eyes opened again. "So did they catch the shooter?"

"I don't think so."

Rocky clicked a button. A machine attached to the IV pole beeped. "Modern medicine," he said. "They let you give yourself your own pain meds these days."

"You must be hurting a lot, huh?"

"Mmm." His eyes drifted closed again. She watched the frown lines leave his forehead as the pain medication did its job.

"I'd give anything to find the guy who did this to you," Jennie murmured. Taking a deep breath, she gathered her things and left.

———

Jennie still had a couple hours before she needed to be at swim practice. She might as well use the time to study. While stopped at a light three blocks from school, Jennie saw an old man in a tattered gray jacket pushing a grocery cart. She swallowed hard remembering the scene in front of the Channel 22 building the night before. She'd seen a vagrant then—an old man, bent and walking with a limp. Why hadn't she put it together before now? The apartment from which the shot was fired had been rented by a crippled old man in a brown coat. The man she'd seen had a brown coat.

The driver behind her honked. Jennie glanced up. The light was green. She made a left and managed to make it into the school's parking lot before she started shaking. The old man who'd walked right by her and the police was the killer. Jennie knew it in her gut. She'd reacted to the strange look in his eyes. She'd seen fear in those eyes. Had it been a fear of being recognized? Why hadn't she been more alert? Why hadn't she made the connection sooner? He'd walked right by the crime scene and no one noticed. Had it been a disguise? Had she seen him before? Had he recognized her?

Jennie hurried inside and made a beeline for the student phone near the mailboxes. She dialed home first, thinking Dad might still be there. Mom answered. "He left about five minutes ago, sweetheart. What's wrong? Are you all right?"

"I'm fine. I just remembered something about last night."

"You should be able to get him on the cell phone."

Dad answered on the first ring. Jennie told him about the old man she'd seen. "Dad, I feel so bad. We could have had him."

"Not your fault, princess. Unfortunately, the guy's disappeared into thin air. John Weed doesn't exist. Phony name and address."

"If it helps, he has blue eyes—I think."

"Right—along with half the population."

"Maybe I can recognize him."

After a long pause, Dad said, "Where are you?"

"At school."

"Good. I don't want you going anywhere alone, do you hear me?"

"Dad—"

"Don't argue with me, Jennie. If this guy recognized you—"

"I'll be careful." A chill swept through her as she remembered his gaze focusing in on hers.

"Good."

"Dad, have you talked to Detective Mallory?"

"Mallory?"

He hadn't. Jennie filled him in on her visit to the abortion clinic and on Lucy's death. "I think it's all connected, Dad. I told him he should tell you."

Silence again. Jennie could almost see him running a hand down his face. "I don't like this. You're too close. No more snooping. No nothing. I don't want you even thinking about this investigation."

"I was just trying to help Annie. . . ."

"No."

"But—"

"Do I have to spell it out for you? Somehow you've gotten yourself entangled in the net this guy's thrown out. I don't know why or how, but I intend to find out. Now, in the meantime, you stay put. Go to swimming and head straight home. No buts."

"Okay. I was going to do that anyway."

After another mini-lecture, Jennie hung up and made her way to the library. There she forced her questions and concerns about Noreen, Lucy, Debra, and Annie from her mind and tried to focus on her studies.

After school the questions surfaced again when Lisa came up to her in the mail room and told her Annie hadn't been at school that day.

"I'm worried, Jen. She seemed so fragile yesterday."

"I know. Maybe her parents wanted her to stay home."

"I called her at lunch, but no one answered."

"Her parents both work." Jennie pulled the papers out of her box.

"Hey, I was hoping to find you two here." Gavin closed in on them. "Jennie, I need a ride to the pool."

"Sure, but why are you going there? We're not having a meet or anything."

"Yeah, you are. It's an exhibition meet with St. Mary's."

Jennie groaned. "How'd I miss that? I'd better move it."

"What about Annie?" Lisa slammed her mailbox door shut.

"What about her?" Gavin shoved his glasses back against his nose.

"I'm worried. She seemed so depressed. And she didn't come to school today."

"I think I know why." Gavin opened his mailbox and pulled the contents out. "She and Shawn had another fight last night."

"Oh no."

"Yeah. Shawn is pretty bummed out about it. All he did was talk to Charity yesterday after school."

Jennie chewed on her lower lip. "Lisa, maybe you should just go by her house on your way home. Didn't you drive today?"

"No. Mom dropped me off. I was hoping you'd drive to her place before the meet."

"I can't be late again or I'll get kicked off the team."

Lisa brightened. "I have an idea. Why don't you drop me off at home on the way to the pool. Hopefully I can borrow the car and go over there."

"I'm not sure you should go alone. There's been another murder, and someone shot at Debra last night."

"Oh no. Is she okay?"

"She is, but Rocky wasn't so lucky." Jennie filled them in on the latest news. "If I'm right and all this is connected, Annie could be in danger."

"Why don't we go by Annie's now?" Lisa said. "It's on the way. We have enough time."

Jennie glanced at her watch. She still had forty minutes to get to the pool. "Okay, as long as we don't have to stop anywhere else."

Driving into Annie's neighborhood, the first thing Jennie noticed was the squad car sitting in the driveway beside a black Lincoln. A lump lodged itself in her throat. Could Annie have been the next victim?

"The police . . . oh, Jennie." Lisa undid her seat belt and opened the door the moment Jennie stopped at the curb.

Gavin climbed out and waited for Jennie to join them. "There's only one car. It can't be too serious."

And no crime scene tape. "Let's hope so."

They hurried up the driveway and took the path to the front door. Lisa rang the doorbell.

One long minute later, the door opened. Mrs. Ellison, Annie's grandmother, pushed open the screen door. "Can I help you?"

"We're friends of Annie's," Jennie said. "She wasn't in school today and—"

"You were here the other day, weren't you?" Mrs. Ellison stepped outside and closed the door behind her.

"Yes. I'm Jennie McGrady. Um . . . is Annie okay? We were worried about her."

A frown deepened the lines on her tanned face. "I wish I knew. She's gone again. Jeanette asked me to come by to check on her when she didn't answer the phone. Annie left a note. My husband is talking with the police right now."

"I should call my mom to see if she showed up at my house again."

"I doubt that very much, Jennie." Mrs. Ellison's gray-green eyes welled up with tears. "The note said she wasn't coming back. I'm afraid . . . I'm afraid she may have committed suicide."

# 23

By six-thirty Friday night, Jennie was ready to quit swimming and drop her extra classes. Never had she worked so hard or been so exhausted. Though she'd managed to turn in the rough draft of her science project, her schedule was packed, and Jennie's biggest concern was Annie. She'd been missing for three days. The only good news was that they hadn't found her body. Hopefully that meant she was still alive.

With hospital visits to Rocky, school, and swimming, Jennie hadn't had any time to check into Annie's disappearance. Not that she could. Her father had forbidden her to even bring the subject up. Jennie still harbored terrifying thoughts that Annie's disappearance had something to do with the bombing of the abortion clinic, Noreen's and Lucy's deaths, and the attempt on Debra's life.

Jennie planned to visit Annie's parents on Saturday afternoon after she stopped to see Rocky. She also wanted to talk to Annie's grandfather. Dr. Ellison had been in practice for about thirty years. He'd told Mom he would give her the names of some doctors who did abortions. Mom didn't need the list, but Jennie did. Maybe Dr. Ellison knew which doctors had worked at the Marsh Street Clinic when Annie was born. Dad had told her not to get involved, but she couldn't just do nothing. Besides, it wouldn't hurt to find out who in town did abortions, would it? She was walking a fine line and knew it, but she told herself she could use the information in her science project.

Jennie was just starting to work on the final draft of her project when the phone rang.

"Jennie, this is Debra," the harried voice said. "I need to talk with you. Can you have dinner with me tonight?"

"Dinner? Um . . . I guess so. What's up?" Debra had gone home, but surprisingly, she'd taken Dad's advice and not appeared on television. She had, however, gone back to work.

"I can't explain it over the phone. Just come to the studios. We can go from there."

"I can't. Dad said he didn't want me going anywhere alone."

"Then I'll pick you up. Will that work?"

"I suppose."

"Good. I'll be there in . . . say, twenty minutes?"

"Sure." Jennie hung up and hurriedly brushed her teeth and hair, then scribbled a quick note to her parents. Mom and Dad were going out to dinner at McDonald's and taking Nick to see a movie. Jennie had opted not to go with them. She was glad now that she hadn't and felt certain her parents wouldn't mind her going out with Debra. She was, after all, still under police protection.

While she waited, Jennie let all the details of the investigation tumble back to the foreground of her mind. She hadn't been able to catch Debra long enough to talk to her about the specifics of her abortion. Jennie's intuition burned to link Debra and Annie together. Unfortunately, she needed proof.

She'd never been able to come up with a logical explanation as to why Noreen Smith had placed Annie in that trash bin and called from the pay phone. She still believed there had been a live fetus and that for some reason Noreen hadn't wanted the clinic, herself, or the doctor implicated. So she did the only thing possible that would still give the baby a fighting chance.

That baby, of course, was Annie. Jennie also felt certain that the woman in the phone booth with the white shoes was not Annie's mother, but Noreen Smith. Unfortunately, everything was speculation. As far as she knew, the police had no substantial leads regarding Noreen's death. When she'd asked her father if Lucy's and Noreen's deaths were linked, he'd said, *"It doesn't look that way."* Lucy, Dad had told her after she'd asked him for the umpteenth time, had committed suicide by taking an overdose of prescription drugs. She'd even left a suicide note. There had been nothing in either Noreen's or Lucy's home to indicate that the two had kept contact over the years. According to Lucy's family, she'd been despondent since the Marsh Street Clinic bombing and worried about finding a job.

Still, Jennie held on to her original suspicions. Now she was finally going to have a chance to question Debra. Maybe the missing puzzle pieces would join to form the picture she'd been putting together all along—that Debra was Annie's mother.

*What if you're wrong, McGrady?* Jennie reminded herself. A strange kind of anxiety filled Jennie's spirit. She hated being wrong. Gladys could have been mistaken about the woman not being Annie's mother. As Dad had said, *"We have no proof. It's entirely possible that the mother was a nurse."*

"Thanks for agreeing to go with me, Jennie," Debra said when Jennie climbed into the passenger seat of Debra's beige Cadillac. As usual, Debra was wearing a fashionable suit—this one in a rich blue that brought out the blue in her eyes.

"No problem." Jennie glanced into the backseat, then out to the road. "Where's your police escort?"

"I decided I didn't need one anymore." She backed down the drive. "I thought we'd go to Antonio's. Do you like Italian?"

"Sure. Aren't you scared? I mean, you were almost killed, and they haven't found the guy yet. And why aren't you wearing your disguise?"

"I don't always wear it. Besides, there haven't been any more attempts on my life. I feel terrible about Officer Rockwell. He almost died trying to save me. I'd just as soon not have anyone else hurt. Anyway, I figure if it's my time to go . . . But let's not talk about that."

Twenty minutes later, they entered Antonio's, where Debra had made reservations. They were seated at a table near the back of the restaurant.

Feeling underdressed and out of place in her jeans and T-shirt, Jennie settled her jacket over the back of the chair. "Um . . . I guess I should have changed."

"You're fine." Debra spread a white linen napkin over her lap and picked up the menu. Jennie did the same.

After choosing lasagna and salad, Jennie set the menu aside.

"What did you want to talk to me about, Jennie?" Debra closed her menu as well.

"Me? What makes you think I wanted to talk? You're the one who called me."

Debra smiled. "Yes, I did, but I can tell the feeling is mutual."

"I do want to ask you some questions, but you go first."

"I'd like to see the killer caught," Debra went on. "I was hoping we could work together."

"Work together?"

"Yes. I've been doing some investigating on my own. Nothing against your father, Jennie, but I'm not happy with the way things are going."

"He caught the serial killer."

She snorted. "Right—the guy practically gave himself up. I think the more dangerous one is still out there somewhere, and . . . well, I don't like being a victim."

"I don't know what I can do. Dad hasn't told me much. Besides, I'm not supposed to be involved."

"Maybe not, but I know you've been investigating on your own. So have I. I know you went to the Park Hill Clinic and talked to Ellen. She gave you Lucy's phone number, and now Lucy is dead."

"How did you—"

"Make the connection? The same way you did. I followed the same trail you were on. Talked to the woman who owned the store and started digging into Noreen's life. In fact, I went to her home—an upscale condo on the waterfront."

Jennie grimaced. "That was on my list of stuff to do before Dad got paranoid."

"You can save yourself the trouble. Like I said, if we share information, maybe we can figure this thing out."

Jennie hesitated. On one hand, Dad might be mad. On the other, maybe Debra had information the police could use. "Okay, on one condition. Whatever we dig up we give to my dad."

Debra smiled. "That's exactly what I had in mind."

"What did you find out about Noreen?"

"I was suspicious about her living in such a nice place on the salary she was pulling in. A neighbor said she'd come into an inheritance when her parents died. I managed to get ahold of her bank statements—"

"How?"

"Computers are wonderful tools, Jennie, and when you know someone . . . Let's just say I have a friend who feeds me information. What matters is that Noreen's deposits included quarterly payments of $10,000 up until her death. I think she was blackmailing someone. The blackmailer got tired of the game and killed her."

"But who?"

"Paul Phillips, maybe? He was on duty at the hospital the day Annie was brought in. He and his wife were desperate for a baby. Suppose he and his wife stole a baby out of the nursery and the trash thing was just a setup. . . ." She frowned. "But that wouldn't work, would it? There were no missing babies, just an extra one."

Jennie licked her lips. "Debra, I need to ask you something."

"Shoot."

"It's about your abortion. Can you tell me where you had it?"

"Where?" She frowned. "In Portland."

"Yes, but where? Did you go to a clinic? If so, which one?"

Debra picked up her water glass and took a drink. She set it down before answering. "It was a long time ago. I don't remember. Why do you want to know?"

Jennie wasn't certain she believed her. "It might be important."

"Can I take your order?" The waiter, a tall young man in a white shirt and black tie, wrote down their selections and left.

"I left Portland the day after I graduated from high school. I couldn't bear to stay here. Not after . . . I thought maybe going to another town, meeting other people, might help. It didn't. I've lived just about everywhere during the last sixteen years. Finally I decided I needed to come back here and face my fears."

"Why were you looking into Noreen Smith's death?" Jennie

asked. "Did you recognize her? Was she working at the clinic where you had the abortion?"

Debra shook her head. "No, I . . ."

She was lying again. Maybe Debra was more closely related to the death of the two women and the bombing of the clinic than Jennie had originally thought. Debra had been away for a long time. She harbored guilt about having an abortion. Had she come back to seek revenge? Had she killed Noreen and torn her own place apart? She could have put on men's shoes to make it look like a man had been there. Had she hired someone to take a shot at Rocky, making it look like the gunman was after her? Had she bombed the clinic?

"Was it the Marsh Street Clinic?" Jennie ran a finger along the handle of her knife.

Debra closed her eyes. "I don't know. Jennie, please. I've spent sixteen years trying to forget. I really don't see any point in talking about it."

"I'm sorry. I know it's painful for you, but I need to ask. How far along were you when you had your abortion?"

"What does that have to do with anything?"

"Debra, please answer me. If my hunch is right, Annie could be your daughter."

"That's impossible. My baby died."

"Maybe. Maybe not. What if your baby survived? What if Noreen Smith was working at the Marsh Street Clinic the day you had the abortion?"

Debra stared at her water glass. "I was seven months along. And, yes, it was at the Marsh Street Clinic."

"What time did you have it done?"

"It was late—after hours. The doctor said he had to do it after hours because he was all booked up. I think it was because he didn't want anyone to know he'd done a late-term."

"Before Annie was found?"

"Maybe—I couldn't say. I remember there being only one nurse."

"Noreen Smith."

"I don't know. And I really don't see how any of this relates." Debra picked up her coffee cup with a shaky hand.

"I think Noreen Smith was working in the Marsh Street Clinic sixteen years ago. I think she's the one who put Annie into the Dumpster and called the police."

"But . . . how can that be? The police were looking for Annie's mother."

"What the police didn't know was that the woman who called them that night was wearing white shoes. Nursing shoes. The clinic was only half a block away from the trash bin. See, I think Noreen Smith was assisting with a late-term abortion that went wrong—or maybe I should say right. Annie was supposed to have been aborted, but she lived. I think Annie is your daughter."

Debra rubbed her forehead. "It can't be."

"Who was your doctor—the one who performed the abortion?"

"I don't remember."

"How can you not remember your doctor?"

"I was very young, Jennie. As I said before, all I wanted to do was forget. I thought my baby was dead. Besides, I only saw the doctor a couple of times."

"Don't you have any records or anything with a name on it? A bill? A receipt?"

"No. Nothing. I threw everything away. I'd give anything to know his name." A hard look passed across her features, then disappeared.

"The records were all destroyed in the bombing," Debra said. "That much the police told me. There was no way to prove Noreen worked there. I imagine that, like us, they're trying to track down other employees. All I've been able to find out was that there was a large turnover."

Over dinner they talked about how they might find out which doctors in town had access to the Marsh Street Clinic. Jennie assured Debra that her father would take care of it.

Debra wasn't listening. "What about your mother's gynecologist?"

"Dr. Ellison doesn't do abortions."

"No, but he could tell us who does. She told me he had been in practice for over thirty years and was nearing retirement.

Maybe he can give us some names."

"Actually, I was going to ask him that tomorrow."

"Why not tonight?"

"I don't think so. My parents don't like me to stay out late."

Jennie could hardly wait to get out of the restaurant. She needed to talk to her dad about Debra's motives. Now it looked as though Debra was using Jennie to track down the doctor who had killed her baby. The more Jennie thought about it, the more sense it made. In a way Jennie hoped she was wrong. She hated thinking Annie's birth mother might be a killer. If indeed Debra was Annie's mother.

They left the restaurant at seven-thirty. Five minutes later, Jennie was sitting in the driver's seat of Debra's car. Which would have been fine if Debra hadn't been sitting next to her holding a gun.

# 24

"Where are we going?" Jennie said, trying to keep her voice calm. Terror edged its way through her body like tentacles of some alien being.

"Just drive. Get on the freeway and head for Lake Oswego."

Jennie focused on getting out of the downtown area. Once they were on the freeway heading south, she tried talking to Debra again. "Why are you doing this? It could ruin your career, and if Annie really is your child . . ."

"She is. I'm sure of that now. A blood test will prove it. The moment I talked to Gladys at that little mom-and-pop place and saw where the Marsh Street Clinic had been, I knew it. The time Annie was found coincides with the time they performed—or I should say botched—the abortion on me. I don't know what happened or who Noreen was blackmailing, but I intend to find out. And when I do . . ."

"You're going to kill the doctor, aren't you?"

"Yes. He destroyed my life—took away my baby. He deserves to die."

"That might be, but you made the choice. Besides, you need to let the—"

"Let the police take care of it? I don't think so. The man has covered his trail too well. He killed Noreen and Lucy and tried to kill me twice."

Jennie gave her a sidelong glance. "You're saying you didn't kill Noreen?"

Debra jerked back, looking as if Jennie had slapped her. "Of course not."

168

"Then why are you holding a gun on me? Why are you making me go with you?"

"I've got to find him, and you're going to help me. Dr. Ellison seems like the most likely person to contact. Like you said, he might know which of his colleagues worked at the clinic."

"Somehow I don't think the gun is going to convince him to tell you anything."

"That's why I brought you. I thought he might be more open to you than me." Debra glanced at the gun as if it were a foreign object. "Oh, you're probably right. I . . . I'm not thinking straight. I shouldn't have forced you to come with me. This entire thing is crazy, Jennie. I have to find the doctor who aborted Annie. I have to know for sure."

"Look." Jennie released a long breath, willing herself to relax. "Let's go back to my house. We'll talk to Dad and—"

"No. You're coming with me. I'm too close to let you run to your daddy and have him mess this up for me. Besides, I need a witness. We're almost there. Take the next exit."

Debra directed her to a posh retirement neighborhood and asked her to pull up to the curb of a single-story home that looked very much like the others. A well-manicured lawn and gardens greeted them. The house bordered a golf course.

"Where are we?"

"At Dr. Ellison's." She waved the gun. "Get out."

"How did you know where he lived?"

"Annie told me."

"Annie . . ." Jennie tipped her head back. "Oh man, you have Annie, don't you?"

"I had to get her away and into a safe place. It's only a matter of time before the murderer tries to kill her too." Debra stepped out of the car and waited for Jennie.

"Where is she?" Jennie undid her seat belt and reached for the car door.

"You'll find out as soon as the danger has passed. Now let's go."

"I think you should leave your gun in the car."

"Why, so you can run off? No way. I've come this far, and I'm not turning back."

"At least put it in your purse. Dr. Ellison looks like he's in pretty good shape. He's likely to attack you first and ask questions later. I don't want anyone getting hurt."

"All right, but don't try to escape. Remember, I have Annie."

At Debra's request, Jennie led the way up the walk and rang the bell. She could have gotten the upper hand—shoved Debra aside and run away. At the moment, however, she felt no real sense of danger. Once inside, she would find a way to let Dr. Ellison know about Debra's gun. Or maybe it would be better to wait until she led her back to Annie.

Dr. Ellison opened the door and stepped aside. "Jennie. Ms. Noble. What a surprise. Do you have news of Annie?"

*Debra has her.* Jennie pleaded with him to read her mind.

"No," Debra said. "Jennie and I wanted to ask you some questions about the day Annie was found."

He gave Jennie a questioning look. "I'm afraid I don't understand."

"May we come in?" Debra nudged Jennie forward.

"Of course. Please have a seat." He gestured toward the curved sectional. The house had been decorated in a southwest flavor with soft tones of peach, turquoise, and beige, with occasional brighter color spots. It matched Dr. Ellison's dark tan, turquoise polo shirt, and khaki shorts.

"Can I get you anything?" He walked over to a bar at the far side of the room.

"No, thanks," Debra said. "Dr. Ellison, let's get right to the point. Jennie and I have been investigating Annie's birth, and we think it was Noreen Smith, not Annie's birth mother, who put her in the trash bin that night."

"Noreen Smith?" He frowned and walked to a cabinet, where he scooped ice out of a bucket and poured himself something from a black bottle.

"The nurse who was murdered a couple of weeks ago." This time it was Jennie who spoke. "We think Annie may be Debra's child."

He set his drink aside. "I still don't follow you."

"Noreen Smith was murdered because of what she knew." Jennie glanced at Debra, who seemed to have spaced out. Since

170

she wasn't making any move toward the gun, Jennie decided to make the most of the interview with Dr. Ellison. She told him about the doctor Debra had seen and how she'd gone in for an abortion on the same night Annie was found in the trash bin. "We're looking for the doctor who performed the abortion on Debra because we think he might be the killer."

"I see. And why have you come to me? I told you before, I don't do abortions."

"I know, but the other day you told my mother that if she were to have an abortion, you would recommend someone. We were hoping you could tell us which doctors might have been working at the Marsh Street Clinic the night Annie was found."

Still standing behind the bar, he rubbed a hand through his silver hair. "That's a tall order. These days I'm lucky to remember my name. I could give you the names of some colleagues who were practicing then, but I doubt it will do you any good. Any baby who lived through an abortion would have been taken to the hospital. I can't imagine any nurse putting one in a Dumpster. Now, I have heard of incidents where a baby is sold on the black market, but—"

"No . . ." Debra whimpered. She stared blankly at a large painting of a younger Dr. and Mrs. Ellison on the opposite wall, then turned a disbelieving look at the doctor. The look of recognition in her eyes turned Jennie's stomach into knots. Dr. Ellison had been Debra's doctor.

The pieces began coming together, but not soon enough. Debra reached into her purse for the gun.

Before she could take it out, Jennie stood, pulling Debra to her feet. She didn't want a confrontation. She and Debra were no match for the doctor. "Um . . . we really should be going." Jennie cleared her throat. "We've taken up enough of your time. If you think of someone who might have been working that night, maybe you could call us."

Debra jerked out of Jennie's grasp and reached into her handbag again.

"No, Debra, don't!" Jennie watched in horror as the gun emerged from the small black bag.

Dr. Ellison proved even more agile than she'd expected. Before Debra could raise the gun, he ripped it out of her hand and turned it on them. Backing away, he ordered them to sit on the couch. "You aren't going anywhere," he growled.

"I told you not to bring the gun." Jennie sagged against the plush cushions. "I'm sorry, Dr. Ellison," Jennie said, still pretending she didn't know about him.

"Save it, Jennie." Dr. Ellison looked extremely sad. "I'd hoped it would stop with Noreen and the clinic. I never meant for anyone to get hurt."

Debra began sobbing.

Dr. Ellison started to reach for her in an empathetic gesture, then stepped back. "I didn't mean for it to happen. I just wanted to do what was best for you and your baby. You were young and unmarried."

"What was best? You let me believe I killed my child. All these years of torment. Do you have any idea what it's like? No, of course you don't. How could you?"

Jennie swallowed back her own tears. "What happened that night, Dr. Ellison? Why was Noreen blackmailing you?"

He seemed surprised. "How could you have known that?"

"It doesn't matter."

He sank into the chair behind him but kept Debra's gun trained on them. "I'm a doctor, Jennie, not a killer. I never wanted to hurt anyone, but I did make a huge mistake. I performed an abortion and walked away from a viable infant."

"You knew the baby was alive, and you . . . you left her?"

There were tears in his eyes—eyes Jennie now recognized as those belonging to the old man she'd seen near the Channel 22 building. He pinched the bridge of his nose. "No . . . I didn't know, not until Noreen called me later that night. Then it was too late to do anything about it. Noreen told me she was cleaning up and heard the baby cry. She asked me what to do. I didn't want the publicity. Even though late-term abortions were legal, most people, including my colleagues, frowned on it, except when the mother's health was in danger. When Noreen came up with the idea of putting the baby in the trash bin and calling the police to report it, I felt nothing but relief. I suggested Paul and Jeanette try to adopt Annie, and they did. I quit doing abortions then. Found I couldn't stomach it anymore. Every time I did one, I'd think of Annie and how close I came to destroying her."

"When did Noreen start blackmailing you?" Jennie asked.

"About a month later. She threatened to go to the authorities and tell them I'd walked out on a viable fetus and that it had been my idea to throw the baby away. She would admit to calling 9-1-1 and come out the hero. It would have ruined my reputation. Had I not paid her off, I stood to lose everything."

"Why didn't you tell me my baby was alive?" Debra seemed more composed now. "She belonged to me, not to your daughter and son-in-law."

"I thought about it, but you were so young and I didn't know how to contact you. Besides, I felt it was better that Annie go to a good home with responsible parents. Annie's had a wonderful life."

"No—you couldn't tell me because the truth would have come out. You had to keep your little secret and your career. Did Paul and Jeanette know?"

He shook his head. "No one did except for Noreen and me."

"What about Lucy?"

"Ah yes, Lucy. She somehow connected Noreen's death with the bombing of the clinic and called me. She remembered that I used to work with Noreen. She'd lost her job and needed money. I wasn't about to get into that kind of trap again. She had a prescription for tranquilizers, and I . . ." He didn't finish—didn't have to. The man was a cold-blooded killer.

"As painful as this is for me, I'm going to have to do away with the two of you as well."

"I wouldn't do that if I were you." Jennie struggled to keep the panic out of her voice. "Debra has Annie hidden somewhere without food or water. If you kill her, you may be killing Annie too."

The agony etched in Dr. Ellison's features spurred Jennie on. He clearly loved Annie, and she doubted he'd do anything to hurt her. "I . . ."

"If you really love her," Jennie went on, "you'll let the truth come out. She needs to know what happened."

"I already know, Jennie."

Jennie's head snapped around at the sound of Annie's voice as she entered the room.

"Annie." Dr. Ellison's shoulder's slumped. He dropped into the chair. "How long have you been there?"

"Long enough."

"I thought you'd been kidnapped."

"No. I've been staying with Debra. I asked her not to tell anyone where I was. But I decided it was time to go home. Mom and Dad were gone, so I came here." She walked toward her grandfather. "If you have to shoot someone, then let it be me. I won't let you hurt Debra and Jennie."

He lowered the gun, dropping it to the floor. "I'm so sorry, Annie. I never meant to hurt you or Debra." He lowered his head to his knees and sobbed.

Jennie shoved herself out of the chair and carefully picked up the gun by the barrel to avoid smudging the fingerprints, then dialed 9-1-1.

# 25

Unable to sleep, Jennie tossed aside her covers and dragged her favorite blanket with her to the window seat. A pale quarter moon hung in the dark sky, lighting her way as she stepped over the clothes she'd taken off and dumped there earlier.

Fluffing up the pillows, Jennie lowered herself onto the wide seat and leaned against the wall. She gazed into the heavens, still wondering how someone as nice as Dr. Ellison seemed to be could have made so many wrong choices. He'd started out doing his best to help people but in the process had made a terrible mistake. He'd put his job and his reputation ahead of saving a life. He'd walked away from a live fetus, a baby. Annie.

Four days had passed since the night he was arrested.

Jennie felt a sense of relief that this chapter was over and life would go on. Annie realized now that the Phillipses were her parents and always would be—they had raised her and loved her as their own. But Annie also planned to get to know Debra, her birth mother.

What still troubled Jennie, and would for a long time, was that Dr. Ellison had gotten off far too easily. In his wake he'd left a devastated widow and daughter. He'd had a fatal heart attack on the way to the police station. His case would never go to trial. Fortunately, Jennie's father had been able to piece things together with her testimony and the evidence he'd found in Dr. Ellison's office.

On the other hand, as her dad had reminded her the night before, he would be facing the toughest Judge of all, God.

*You have to let it go, McGrady,* she scolded herself.

"*Leave it in God's hands.*" That's what Gram had told her when Jennie had spoken to her the night before.

Eventually she'd be able to do that. Jennie took a deep breath and turned her mind to more pleasant things.

Rocky was at home and doing better than anyone expected. Jennie planned to visit him and his sister on her way to school. With his sister in a wheelchair, they'd need help until Rocky was on his feet again.

She had completed her science project and would be entering it in the Science Fair next week. On Saturday she'd go to the Fall Festival. She wouldn't be going with Lisa and Gavin after all. Instead, she'd have her own escort. Ryan was coming!

Jennie smiled as she picked up the gift she'd purchased for him. A model car. A white 1964 Corvette convertible, to be exact. Okay, so maybe it wasn't the real thing.

She chuckled. "It's the thought that counts."

had never been a studious boy, but by sheer force of will he was able to make his mind recall those lessons his schoolmaster had ingrained in him.

*Scritch-scratch. Scritch-scratch. Scritch-scratch.*

Dear God in heaven, this would not do. Maddie looking studious as he droned on only served to distract him. That little furrow between her eyebrows was utterly arousing. Then there was the way her pink tongue stuck out from the corner of her mouth and she concentrated on taking notes… It made him want to lick at it. He had to think of the least arousing thing on earth.

'Mating toads,' he croaked out.

*Scritch—*

'I beg your pardon?'

'Mating toads signal their interest by producing sounds at loud volumes,' he continued. 'Their vocal sacs can amplify….'

Cam had nearly exhausted his knowledge of the mating rituals of frogs and toads when a delicate cough interrupted him.

'*Ahem.*'

'Yes?'

Maddie regarded him. 'It's not that I'm complaining…'

'But?'

'As much as I am impressed by your knowledge of the animal kingdom, I thought we would be engaging in more…practical lessons.' She put her notebook aside. 'Is learning all about animal husbandry necessary?'

His first plan to distract her with useless facts hadn't fooled her, it seemed. So perhaps he had to switch tactics. First, he needed to assess what she did know about flirting. 'Tell me, then. What do you think these lessons should be about?'

'Well.' She stood up, and by instinct he did as well.

'How exactly do I begin flirting? According to Miss Merton, there is a very limited amount of subjects I can discuss with a gentleman. The weather, music, art, general events, the items in a room… But how do those lead to flirting?'

'They do not,' he replied. 'Flirting isn't just talking. Yes, that's a big part of it, but it's not just about what you say, but what you do not say.'

She looked up at him, big eyes eager and earnest. 'How so?'

'The way you look at a man, for example, could be an indication of your interest. When a man is speaking, you should look into his eyes. You must appear that you are eager to hear anything he has to say.'

'Anything?'

Cam smiled to himself. The vexed expression on her face gave him an idea on exactly how to proceed.

He continued. 'Aye. I know these English fops can drone on and on about the silliest thing, but you'll have to endure.' He wondered how long Maddie could keep that up. *She would surely hate it.* And perhaps if he made it sound as terrible as possible, she would give up on this idea of flirting.

'And what else?'

'Well…' He thought for a moment. 'The way you speak with your body is another factor.'

'A body can speak?'

'Aye. Think of it as a kind of language, like French or Italian. Your body language.' It took all of Cam's effort not to stare down at said body. 'It says a lot about you. For example, when you face a gentleman you want to flirt with, try leaning your head towards him.'

'Like this?' She leaned her head forward and came